The Witches of Winged-Horse Mountain

By

Sandra Forrester

BARRON'S

Contents

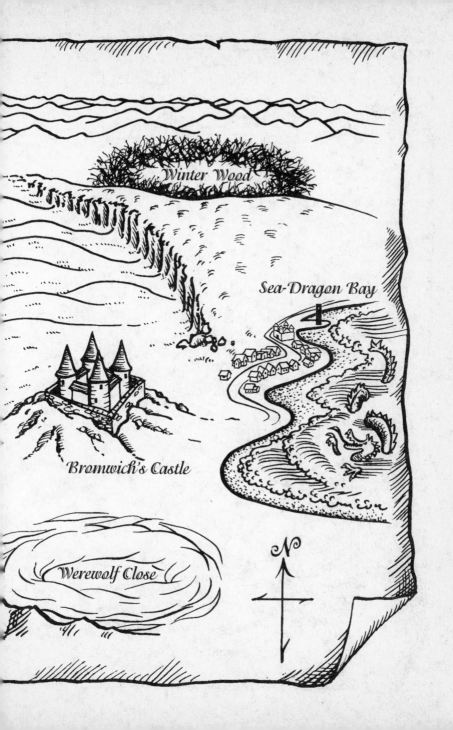

Winter Wood

Sea-Dragon Bay

Bromwich's Castle

Werewolf Close

N

Blood
Mountain

Morven's
House

Hunter's Trail
begins

Winged-
Horse Ranch

Winged-Horse
Mountain

Gnome
Village

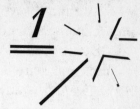

Disturbed and Dangerous!

*T*he dismissal bell rang and students came pouring through the doors of John Greenleaf Whittier Middle School. It was Friday afternoon—the last weekend before final exams—and with summer vacation just around the corner, the always energetic twelve- and thirteen-year-olds seemed to be electrically charged.

Among the first to burst from Whittier's air-conditioned halls into the June heat were Beatrice Bailey and her two friends, Teddy Berry and Cyrus Rascallion. A casual observer probably wouldn't notice anything unusual about the three seventh graders, but everyone in school—indeed, everyone in *town*—knew that Beatrice, Teddy, Cyrus, and their home-schooled friend, Ollie Tibbs, were different from other twelve-year-olds. The four had been called everything from weirdos to witches—although no one had been able to prove the latter, thus far—and their sometimes peculiar behavior had provided many hours of enjoyable gossip for the townspeople. Beatrice and her friends had learned early that being a witch in the mortal world wasn't always easy, but at the moment they were preoccupied with more mundane concerns.

"Exams start Monday," Cyrus said as they left school grounds and started for home, "and I haven't opened a book. Even if I study all weekend, I'll *never* pass math."

Cyrus was small and dark, with vivid blue eyes. He was normally the most easygoing of the four friends, but now his expression was uncharacteristically glum.

"Since when have you started worrying about grades?" Teddy demanded. "As I recall, you were the only kid in nursery school who flunked nap time."

Cyrus scowled at her. "Was it my fault I couldn't go to sleep on command?" he muttered. "And, anyhow, not everyone has a genius IQ like *some people*."

Teddy paused to consider the unintentional compliment. She was petite and pretty, with short brown curls and dark eyes behind oversize wire-rimmed glasses. It was true that she made straight A's, but no one had any idea how hard she studied—or for that matter, how long it took to make her hair look casually windblown, as if she had just run her fingers through it. But Teddy's ambitions went beyond being the brightest—and prettiest—star at J. G. Whittier Middle School; her ultimate goal was to become the greatest witch who had ever lived, and to enjoy all the fame and fortune that went with it.

"*Your* problem," Teddy said to Cyrus, "is you wait till the last minute for everything. Like now. Two days before finals, and you just start thinking about studying."

"He isn't the only one," Beatrice said, her shoulders sagging under the weight of a backpack that held every textbook she owned.

Beatrice was tall and skinny, with pale red hair cut straight across at the shoulder and silky bangs that habitually fell into her green-gold eyes. She blew her bangs aside now, and added, "I haven't been concentrating enough on schoolwork this year."

Teddy and Cyrus knew the reason for this without asking. Beatrice had had a lot on her mind since the Witches' Executive Committee had shown up at her birthday party last October—as they did routinely when a young witch turned twelve—to announce her witch classification. But from the moment those thirteen witches had materialized in the Baileys' living room, everything in Beatrice's life had gone haywire. Instead of giving her the Everyday classification she had expected, they had told Beatrice that she would have to be tested. If she could pass the test, she'd be classified as a Classical witch, which meant they considered her capable of working important magic.

As it turned out, Beatrice's own family history had provided the means to test her magical abilities. Beatrice had learned that one of her ancestors had left his life as a Traditional witch in the Witches' Sphere, shortened the family name of Bailiwick to Bailey, and come to live in the mortal world as a modern Reform witch. Furthermore, the committee had informed Beatrice, it was written in *The Bailiwick Family History* that the eldest female Bailiwick witch in each generation was charged with trying to reverse a two hundred-year-old spell cast by the evil sorcerer Dally Rumpe. And because Beatrice was the eldest female Bailiwick in her generation, her test would be to try to break Dally Rumpe's spell.

Unlike Teddy, Beatrice had no particular desire to be a Classical witch. In fact, she would have been perfectly content with an Everyday classification. But everything happened so quickly, and before she knew it, Beatrice found herself agreeing to the test. When Teddy, Ollie, and Cyrus volunteered to help Beatrice, the committee agreed to reconsider their Everyday classifications, as well. Unfortunately, Beatrice could cast only one kind of spell, as could each of her friends, and yet—somehow!—they had managed to break Dally Rumpe's spell on Winter Wood, Werewolf Close, and, most recently, Sea-Dragon Bay. But there were still two parts of the spell that hadn't been reversed, which meant two more trips into the darkest and most dangerous regions of the Witches' Sphere. Sometimes Beatrice would wake up in a sweat, wondering when their luck would finally run out.

She was frowning now, obviously worried. "I'm so far behind," Beatrice said, "I'll probably fail half my exams."

"But you always get good grades," Teddy assured her. "A's and B's, right?"

"I got a D minus on my American history midterm," Beatrice admitted. "And a D in Spanish. That was right after we came back from Werewolf Close and I was still having awful dreams about werewolves and enchanted fog. And that horrible monster Allbones!" she finished with a shudder.

"Don't forget the snakes and the screaming trees," Cyrus said.

"And the heat and humidity," Teddy murmured. "My hair was a mess."

"I know what you mean," Beatrice said dryly. "A bad hair day can give me nightmares for weeks."

Just then, Amanda Bugg and Olivia Klink caught up with them and fell into step on either side of Beatrice and Teddy, leaving Cyrus to trail behind. Beatrice grimaced. It seemed that Amanda and her crowd had made it their life's mission to pry into every corner of Beatrice's life, hoping to prove that she was up to something scandalous.

"Hello there, Beatrice," Amanda said sweetly. "Do you have exciting plans for the weekend?"

"Not very," Beatrice answered, her voice as stony as her expression.

"That's surprising," Amanda said with a smile that was actually more of a smirk. "I mean, you and your friends are always doing something *interesting*."

Still walking and not bothering to look at Amanda, Beatrice shrugged. "Do you consider studying for finals interesting? Because that's what I'll be doing this weekend."

"Of course you will," Amanda said, her voice suddenly dripping with sympathy. "I've noticed the trouble you've been having in some of our classes. *Actually*," she added brightly, "in *all* of our classes."

Beatrice's face flooded with color and her eyes flashed alarmingly, but before she could speak, Teddy said coldly, "I'm sure Beatrice appreciates your concern, but don't lose any sleep over it. She's going to ace her exams the way she always does."

"She's bound to get at least one A," Olivia chimed in. Then she added slyly, "*Everybody* gets an A in art, as long as they show up."

Amanda shot her friend an approving look and said, "Well, Liv, I guess we'd better not hold them up any longer. Beatrice has a *lot* of studying to do."

Teddy and Cyrus glared at her, and the color in Beatrice's face deepened.

With an especially nasty grin, Amanda flipped her long hair over her shoulder and walked away. A giggling Olivia trotted after her.

"If only I could cast a decent spell," Teddy muttered through clenched teeth, "those two would be *covered* in warts!"

They were approaching Ollie's house when Beatrice had an idea.

"Why don't we go to my house for a snack and a study session till dinner? Ollie can help you with your math, Cyrus."

Cyrus's face lit up. "Yeah! Ollie's really good in math."

"And, Beatrice, I'll quiz you in Spanish and history," Teddy offered.

When they reached Ollie's house, Beatrice looked up and smiled at the weathervane spinning on the roof. It was a witch riding on a broom.

Cyrus knocked on the door and Ollie opened it immediately, as if he had been waiting for them. He was half a head taller than Beatrice and nearly as skinny, with green eyes and a mop of butter-yellow hair. Beatrice thought he was the most handsome boy she had ever seen, not to mention the smartest and the most thoughtful. Sometime during the past year, Beatrice and Ollie had gone from liking each other to *liking* each other, and Beatrice was still a little self-conscious about the subtle change in their friendship.

"Am I glad to see you guys," Ollie said as a huge barn owl swooped down the staircase and waited to take their backpacks. "Mom's had me reading witch history for the past two hours and I'm about to slip into a coma. Come on in."

"Actually," Beatrice said, "we were hoping you could come over to my house and help Cyrus study for exams. We'll feed you," she added with a grin.

"Sounds good to me," Ollie answered cheerfully. "Is math still giving you trouble?" he asked Cyrus.

"*Everything's* giving me trouble," Cyrus replied, sounding a little desperate. "But math's the worst."

On the way to her house, Beatrice told Ollie about her dismal mid-term grades, and Cyrus explained how the whole semester in math had been reduced to a blur of swirling equations that haunted his dreams. By the time they reached Beatrice's yard, Ollie had nearly succeeded in convincing them that all was not lost.

Beatrice's house was big and old and white, like most of the other houses on the street. Except the Bailey house had brilliant lime-green shutters and three glass witch balls in the living room window that flashed blue and green and ruby red in the late afternoon sun. Since witches love to make a statement, Mrs. Bailey had always dreamed of painting the whole house lime green, with turquoise and hot pink trim. But Reform witches living in the mortal world have to rein in their more indiscreet impulses, and the house had remained white.

As they climbed the steps to the porch, Beatrice dug around in the pocket of her shorts and came up with nothing but lint.

"Forgot my key," she muttered, "and Mom and Dad won't be home till 6:30."

"You lock your doors now?" Ollie asked in surprise.

Beatrice nodded. "Mom came home one day and found Chester Sidebottom snooping around the kitchen," she said. "As a matter of fact, there he is spying on us now."

Beatrice's friends followed her gaze across the street and saw a round-faced little boy staring at them from behind an azalea bush. When he realized they had spotted him, Chester ran inside the house and slammed the door behind him.

"He's the one who told his parents that he saw your father flying," Teddy recalled.

Ollie raised an eyebrow. "I didn't know your father could fly."

"He was trying to paint the living room ceiling," Beatrice said, "but the spell backfired—as most of our spells do—and he shot across the room like a rocket."

They all laughed, but gently. None of them had reason to feel superior when it came to magic.

"Now back to our immediate problem," Teddy said. "How do we get into the house?"

"I could walk down to the garden center and get a key from Mom," Beatrice replied.

"You don't need to do that," Cyrus said. "I'll shrink myself and slide in through the letter slot."

"Good idea," Beatrice answered. Then her brows drew together in concern. "I can lift you up to the slot, but it's a long drop on the other side."

"You have a carpet runner in the hall, don't you?" Cyrus said. "That should break my fall."

He walked over to the door and started to mumble:

By the mysteries, one and all,
Make me shrink from tall to small.
Cut me down to inches three,
As my will, so mote it be.

Instantly, Cyrus began to shrink smaller and smaller, until he was only three inches tall. He threw his head back and looked up at Beatrice.

"Okay," Cyrus said in a tiny voice that fit his new size, "hoist me up. And somebody hold the slot open."

Ollie raised the brass flap of the letter slot. Beatrice stooped so that Cyrus could climb into her outstretched hand, then lifted him gently to the opening.

Cyrus scooted over to sit on the edge of the slot, his feet dangling inside the house. "Well, this is it," he said, and jumped.

They heard a dull thud when Cyrus hit the rug.

"Cyrus," Beatrice called out, "are you okay?"

"I'm fine," came Cyrus's faint reply. "Wait a second while I make myself big again."

A moment later, the front door swung open and a full-size Cyrus was grinning at them.

"Thanks," Beatrice said to Cyrus as she, Teddy, and Ollie trooped into the entry hall. "That spell sure does come in handy."

At that moment, a large, long-haired mop of a cat that was predominantly black, with dashes of orange and white, leaped from the hall table into Beatrice's arms. Beatrice looked down into the cat's green-gold eyes that bore a striking resemblance to her own, and smiled.

"Did you miss me, Cayenne?" Beatrice murmured.

Cayenne's answering purr was gravelly and loud, reminiscent of a snowblower.

"I thought the vet put her on a diet," Teddy said, eyeing the cat's ample girth.

"She's lost weight," Beatrice answered defensively. "Not a *lot* of weight, but some."

Ollie grinned. "Cayenne isn't fat," he said, scratching the cat's neck the way she liked it. "You just have big bones, don't you, girl?"

"Speaking of diets," Cyrus said as he headed toward the kitchen, "I haven't had anything to eat since lunch, and I'm starving."

Beatrice made sandwiches and brought out bags of chips and cookies. After everyone's appetite was satisfied, Ollie opened Cyrus's math book.

"When did you start falling behind?" Ollie asked as he flipped toward the back of the book.

"Uh—maybe we'd better begin with Chapter One," Cyrus answered.

Teddy raised her eyebrows and Cyrus scowled at her.

"*Teddy,*" Beatrice said before an argument could erupt, "why don't you help me with my Spanish dialogues?" She thrust an open book into Teddy's hands. "You read the Spanish part and I'll try to translate it into English."

Twenty minutes later, Beatrice was still struggling with the first dialogue and Cyrus was fuming because Ollie wouldn't give him the answer to a math problem.

"I told you how to do it," Ollie said. He was beginning to sound annoyed, which was unusual for Ollie. "If I give you the answer, you won't learn anything."

"Why don't we take a break?" Teddy suggested.

"Good idea," Beatrice said with relief, and slammed her Spanish book shut. "Sorry, Teddy, but my mind keeps wandering. And I need to water the lawn, anyway. Dad just put down grass seed."

"I'll help," Ollie said, starting for the back door.

"We don't have to go outside," Beatrice told him. She walked to the window and began to chant:

> Circle of magic, hear my plea,
> Gentle rain,
> Falling free,
> This, I ask you, bring to me.

As soon as she uttered the final word, a steady rain began to fall outside the window.

Beatrice turned back to her friends. "Thirty minutes should be enough," she said. "Will you remind me to turn it off?"

Ollie grinned. "I didn't think about your weather spells. I have to use a sprinkler."

"So do you guys want to study some more?" Teddy asked.

"Let's look at *The Bailiwick Family History* first," Ollie said, "and see if it's been updated since we broke the spell on Sea-Dragon Bay."

Teddy seemed to come alive at that. "Good idea, Ollie. And we can read about where we're going next."

"The Witches' Executive Committee hasn't told us we'll be going back to the Sphere," Beatrice reminded her.

"They never do till the last minute," Teddy responded.

"And they always wait for a mortal school break," Cyrus said, "so they'll probably have us leave next weekend after exams."

Teddy was studying Beatrice's face with a worried expression. "Don't tell me you're still hoping they'll cancel the test," she said. "They *can't!* Not after we've managed to break three parts of Dally Rumpe's spell. And what have you got against becoming a Classical witch, anyway? Even if it isn't your dream, the rest of us want a chance to redeem ourselves."

Beatrice sighed. "I know, and I wish I could be as excited as you are about all this. But even if we're able—by some miracle—to break the other two parts of Dally Rumpe's spell, I know in my heart I'm never going to be a great witch. So I feel like such a *fraud.* A Classical classification should be reserved for witches who really *are* great."

Teddy was frowning, obviously not liking what she was hearing. "But you didn't ask for the test. The Witches' Executive Committee came to *you,* remember?"

"Only because Dr. Featherstone was determined for me to prove myself," Beatrice answered, a hint of stubbornness creeping into her voice. "When we found out that she and my mother had been friends when they were young, I started to wonder about her motives. Then when the whole story came out—when I realized that Dr. Featherstone felt guilty for not being able to help my mother become Classical—it all made sense. She's just trying to make it up to my mom."

"Who cares *why* the committee decided to test you?" Teddy replied impatiently. "And, anyway, you promised to see this through because you said you owed it to the Bailiwicks—to Bromwich and his daughters. Well, as you know, we've only freed three of the girls so far. Bromwich and his fourth daughter are still Dally Rumpe's captives."

"I *will* see it through," Beatrice said quickly. "But if we manage to survive to the end, and the committee offers me a Classical classification, I don't know if I'll take it or not."

Teddy looked genuinely baffled. "We've been best friends since we were four years old," she said, "and I *still* don't understand you. But it's your decision. As for me, when they offer to change my Everyday classification to Classical, I won't *have* to think about it! I'll already be applying to the best witch academy in the Sphere."

The others laughed, even Beatrice. "Okay, Teddy," she said, still grinning, "I won't ruin your chance of becoming rich and famous. I just hope you're still alive to give all those autographs."

They gathered in the living room around Mr. Bailey's desk and Beatrice picked up a thick book bound in black leather. Its binding was cracked and faded with age, and on the spine was printed *The Bailiwick Family History*.

As Beatrice flipped through the pages, several large black beetles fell from the book to the top of the desk. Cayenne pounced with the grace of a panther, but when she lifted her paw, nothing was there.

"You might as well give up," Beatrice told the cat. "They're protected by magic or something."

Beatrice blew her bangs aside and looked down at the book. "Okay, here it's telling what a wise and powerful sorcerer Bromwich of Bailiwick was," Beatrice said, her eyes skimming the page, "and how he had four daughters—Rhona, Innes, Ailsa, and Morven. Then it tells how an equally powerful, but evil, sorcerer named Dally Rumpe wanted the kingdom of Bailiwick for himself—" Beatrice drew her breath in sharply and looked up at her friends with startled eyes. "The book never mentioned that Bromwich and Dally Rumpe were brothers. We didn't find that out till we went to Sea-Dragon Bay. But it's included now. Listen!"

Everyone moved closer, as surprised as Beatrice by the change in the history.

"'*Dalbert Bailiwick (a.k.a. Dally Rumpe) developed bitter feelings toward his younger brother,*'" Beatrice read, "'*when Bromwich inherited the kingdom of Bailiwick and Dalbert was left nothing but an ancient book of spells. Breaking all ties with the Bailiwicks, the irate Dalbert changed his name to Dally Rumpe (Rumpe being his mother's maiden name) and retreated to a cave in the mountains, where he lived for many years, studying the book of spells and making the acquaintance of ghouls, evil imps, and other disreputable creatures. When he felt that he was powerful enough to claim the kingdom of Bailiwick and seek his revenge against Bromwich, Dally Rumpe cast a spell on the kingdom. Something went horribly wrong with the spell, leaving Bailiwick split into five parts. Bromwich was imprisoned in the dungeon of his own castle, while each of his four daughters was confined in one of the four remaining regions.*'"

"We know all that," Teddy said impatiently. "What does it say about us?"

Beatrice's eyes darted down the page. "Oh, here it is. *'As the eldest female Bailiwick witch in her generation, Beatrice Bailiwick is responsible for reversing Dally Rumpe's spell on the five regions of Bailiwick, which will result in freeing Bromwich and his four daughters from their captivity and reuniting the five regions into one kingdom. To date, Beatrice and her three friends, Teddy Berry, Ollie Tibbs, and Cyrus Rascallion (with the help of Beatrice's cat-familiar Cayenne) have broken the spell on Winter Wood, Werewolf Close, and Sea-Dragon Bay.'* "

Teddy was peering over Beatrice's shoulder. "Good! They spelled my name right."

"It's neat the way the book stays current all by itself," Cyrus said. "Is there any more about us?"

Beatrice turned the page. "It talks about where we'll be going next," she said.

"Read it!" Teddy exclaimed, and Ollie and Cyrus nodded eagerly.

Beatrice hesitated. "This is the part Dr. Meadowmouse always reads when the Witches' Executive Committee comes," she said.

"But it's *your* family history," Cyrus pointed out.

"And the book's in *your* living room," Teddy added. "I'm sure it's okay for you to read it or the committee would have locked it up."

That made sense to Beatrice. "Okay," she said, and her eyes dropped back to the book. "*'Next, Beatrice and her friends will travel to Blood Mountain in the western region of Bailiwick. The dominant element here is fire, resulting in a land that is excessively hot and dry. A crimson sun that never sets casts a red hue on the rugged mountain, which rises high above a desert landscape dotted with cacti and other less formidable mountains.'"*

Teddy frowned. "We'll need a strong sunblock."

"At least there won't be sea monsters, like the ones in Sea-Dragon Bay," Cyrus said.

"Sea monsters weren't the worst of it," Teddy said darkly. "I'd rather face the most deadly sea serpent in the world than deal with Miranda Pengilly again." She glanced quickly at Beatrice. "Sorry," Teddy muttered, "I know she's your cousin, but she really is evil, Beatrice."

"Misguided, anyway," Ollie said tactfully.

"She's *horrible*," Cyrus declared, his expression unrelenting. "Think of all the terrible things she did to us—like making our hot-air balloon crash into Sea-Dragon Bay, and causing me to sprain my ankle, and sending those rats after Beatrice—oh, and nearly causing Ollie to drown."

"What about her giving me witch fever?" Teddy demanded. "You don't know what humiliation is until you've spent forty-eight hours with your face as yellow as a sunflower and covered in boils."

Beatrice nodded sympathetically, holding back a smile. At the time, Teddy's startling appearance had seemed like the least of their problems. But Teddy was so vain, she wasn't likely to ever forget her bout with witch fever.

"And Miranda did all that just because she thought *she* should be the one to break Dally Rumpe's spell, and not Beatrice." Cyrus snorted with contempt. "When the book clearly says that a Bailiwick has to do it—and her name is Pengilly."

"I *do* understand how she felt," Teddy said grudgingly. "If I were Miranda, and a mere technicality was keeping me from the fame I thought I deserved, I wouldn't be happy about it, either. But turning me into a *freak?*" Horror showed plainly on Teddy's pretty face. "That was totally uncalled for!"

"None of us has to worry about Miranda anymore," Ollie reminded them. "Not since Beatrice's great-uncle Xenos sent her to that school for troubled witches."

"That's true," Cyrus replied. "Maybe they'll keep her locked up for a long time."

It was then that Beatrice said quietly, "Miranda *did* save my life."

Teddy opened her mouth to protest, but Beatrice said hastily, "I know, she was working with Dally Rumpe and she came close to killing us all. But in the end, Miranda risked her own life to stand up to him and save mine. I won't forget that."

"Neither will I," Ollie said. "I just hope The Rightpath School will help her learn to make better choices."

"*Sure,*" Teddy said sarcastically. "After a year with all those witch delinquents, she'll probably come out ten times worse!"

Beatrice looked down at the open book in her hands, her thoughts drifting from her cousin to another relative who was far more terrifying in Beatrice's estimation. Since Dally Rumpe and Bromwich were brothers, that meant that Beatrice was also related to the evil sorcerer. It still made Beatrice shudder when she remembered that Dally Rumpe's blood was running through her own veins.

"So finish reading the part about Blood Mountain," Teddy said. "What kinds of terrifying things are we going to face in the desert?"

Just then they heard a car door slam.

"Mom and Dad are home," Beatrice said, and closed *The Bailiwick Family History* gratefully. "Can you guys stay for dinner?"

When Mr. and Mrs. Bailey entered the kitchen, they found the four clearing textbooks and papers from the table. Hamish and Nina Bailey were both tall and skinny like their daughter, but Beatrice's father had thinning dark hair, while her mother's short bob was the same pale red as Beatrice's. Mr. and Mrs. Bailey were wearing identical khaki pants and forest-green polo shirts with *Bailey Nursery & Garden Center* embroidered across the front.

"I hope you're all hungry," Mr. Bailey said heartily. He was carrying several large paper bags that emitted an enticing aroma.

Mrs. Bailey kissed the top of her daughter's head and looked fondly at the other three. "We decided to try that new Greek place. You know, Beatrice, it's next door to the cleaners."

Mr. Bailey had placed the bags in the center of the table and was taking out Styrofoam containers. He opened one and sniffed.

"Ummm . . . spanakopita, gemista, and a Greek salad."

Mrs. Bailey was opening another container. "And we have gyros—and loukoumades for dessert."

Everyone looked delighted except Cyrus. "This is almost as bad as witch food," he said morosely, and the others laughed.

Mrs. Bailey smiled at him. "I thought you might be here, Cyrus, and I know what a meat-and-potatoes kind of guy you are, so . . ." She lifted the lid of another container. "Two cheeseburgers with ketchup, mustard, and onions, and one large French fry."

Cyrus sighed happily. "Thanks, Mrs. B. You're the best!"

"Okay," Mrs. Bailey said, "everybody wash up and dig in before the food gets cold."

They were all sitting around the table, filling their plates and exclaiming over how good everything looked, when the doorbell rang.

"Now who can that be?" Mrs. Bailey wondered aloud.

"I'll go see," Beatrice volunteered.

She dropped some bits of lamb onto Cayenne's plate and then hurried down the hall toward the front of the house. Beatrice was thinking that Amanda Bugg might have stopped by, as she did occasionally, to see if she could catch the Baileys dancing naked around a bonfire or something.

But it wasn't Amanda ringing the bell. Or any other mortal. When Beatrice opened the door, her mouth fell open in surprise. Then she smiled, delighted to see her great-uncle Xenos Bailiwick standing there.

"Uncle Xenos," Beatrice said, "what a terrific surprise! Mom and Dad will be so happy to see you. We've told them all about you."

Xenos Bailiwick hugged Beatrice and then stood back to look at her. He was a small, distinguished-looking man in gray witch robes, with salt-and-pepper hair and intelligent dark eyes. Beatrice knew that her uncle was as fond of her as she was of him, but she could tell that this was more than a casual family visit. In fact, Beatrice realized as she studied his face, her great-uncle appeared deeply troubled.

Suddenly aware of what the neighbors would think if they saw a man in long robes on the Baileys' front porch, Beatrice drew him gently inside.

"What's wrong?" Beatrice asked, and her heart began to beat faster.

"It's Miranda," Xenos said without preamble. "She's run away from The Rightpath School and no one knows where she is."

Beatrice felt a sick sensation in her stomach. "Maybe she's on her way to see you," Beatrice suggested hopefully.

Xenos shook his head. "No, she could have been home in a few hours, and she's been missing for three days. Beatrice, I'm afraid she might be coming here."

Beatrice let her breath out slowly. "To do something to me, you mean?" Her voice was unsteady. She cleared her throat and added, "I don't think Miranda would do that. She's changed."

Xenos's shoulders dropped wearily. "I don't *want* to believe that she would," he said. Then he spread his hands wide, appearing bewildered. "At this point, I don't know *what* to think. Because of her former association with Dally Rumpe, Miranda's disappearance is being reported on every news program in the Sphere. But she was never a true ally of that no-good sorcerer," he burst out, "and she's only thirteen—little more than a child! But to hear those reporters, you'd think she's every bit as evil as he is."

Beatrice patted Xenos's shoulder, not knowing what to say. It was true that she had always defended Miranda, not believing that her own cousin could mean her serious harm. But now, Beatrice wasn't so sure. After being locked up for three months in what amounted to a reform school for witches, had Miranda begun to resent Beatrice even more? Could it be that her cousin really *was* out to get her?

"In those news reports," Xenos was saying, his face appearing haggard and gray, "they're calling Miranda's disappearance an *escape*, and they're warning viewers not to approach her." His dark eyes suddenly filled with tears. "Beatrice, they're saying my granddaughter is presumed to be disturbed and dangerous!"

2

The Heebie-jeebies

When Beatrice and Xenos came into the kitchen, Teddy, Ollie, and Cyrus greeted him warmly.

"Mom and Dad," Beatrice said, "this is Uncle Xenos from Sea-Dragon Bay."

Mr. Bailey leaped to his feet with a delighted smile. "Uncle Xenos," he said, reaching for the older man's hand, "it's a pleasure to meet you."

Mrs. Bailey stood and gave Xenos a big hug. "Beatrice and her friends have told us how kind you were to them," she said. "I hope you've come for a long visit so we can thank you properly."

"Actually, I have to get back to the Witches' Sphere right away." He glanced at Beatrice. "I just came to warn your daughter."

The smiles on Mr. and Mrs. Bailey's faces froze. Teddy, Ollie, and Cyrus looked alert and wary.

"Warn Beatrice about what?" Mr. Bailey asked.

Beatrice glanced from her father's questioning face to her mother's anxious one. "Remember me telling you about Miranda Pengilly?" Beatrice asked them.

"The girl who caused so much trouble," said. Then her cheeks turned pink and she lo at Xenos. "I'm sorry," she said. "Miranda's daughter, isn't she?"

Xenos waved his hand to brush aside her apology. "Yes, she is, and her parents and I have made a real mess of it. But she's young, and I had hoped there was still a chance to rehabilitate her."

Teddy was staring hard at Xenos. "She's run away from that school, hasn't she?" Teddy asked, her tone faintly accusing.

"It would appear so," Xenos said stiffly.

"No one knows where Miranda is," Beatrice said, "but Uncle Xenos thinks she might be coming here."

Mrs. Bailey's expression changed to one of alarm, while Ollie and Cyrus's eyes grew rounder. Teddy didn't appear the least bit surprised.

"She's probably still holding a grudge against you," Teddy said to Beatrice.

"But she's Beatrice's *cousin*," Mrs. Bailey protested. "And even though she made things difficult for all of you, she did end up saving Beatrice's life. I can't believe she'd try to hurt you now."

A hint of a smile appeared on Xenos's lips. "I can see where Beatrice's loyalty to family comes from," he said. Then he sighed. "I really must get back and see if anyone's heard from Miranda. I'll be in touch when I know more," he said to Mr. and Mrs. Bailey. Then he added to Beatrice, "As for you, young lady, promise me that you'll be very careful."

After Xenos had left, no one felt like eating, even Cyrus. Beatrice and Teddy began to clear the table, and

. Bailey said, "What we all need is a nice soothing cup
ﬧ catmint tea."

"I'll fix it," Ollie said, and reached for a teakettle.

After filling the kettle with water, Ollie began to
chant:

> Heat of flame, heat of fire,
> Give to me my one desire.
> Boil this water, bubbling free,
> As my will, so mote it be!

The water in the kettle began to boil.

Beatrice and her friends had carried their cups of tea
outside and settled into canvas chairs on the back porch.
Cayenne was lying on her back in Beatrice's lap. Beatrice
scratched the cat's belly as she watched the sun disappear
behind the trees.

"I knew locked doors and fences wouldn't keep
Miranda from coming after us," Teddy said. "And I don't
think she'll let family ties get in the way, either. She's
probably meeting with Dally Rumpe right now."

"Or she could be out there," Cyrus said, staring wide-
eyed into the gathering dusk, "spying on us."

"I seriously doubt that," Beatrice said, sounding
relaxed and unconcerned. But even so, a shiver ran up her
spine at the thought of Miranda hiding nearby, watching
their every move.

Beatrice's eyes scanned the yard, finally coming to rest on the tangle of ferns and blackberry bushes that grew wild along the back of their property. Seeing something move in one of the bushes, her body tensed and she leaned forward for a better look.

"What was that rustling sound?" Ollie asked.

"There's something in those bushes," Beatrice whispered. "Teddy, can you work your spell?"

"Sure," Teddy answered, and then she began to chant:

> Candle, bell, and willow tree,
> Who is there to spy on me?
> Use your magic for our side,
> Show us who would wish to hide.

Suddenly, the blackberry bushes sprang apart, revealing a large brown rabbit chewing on a mouthful of grass.

Beatrice slumped back in her chair, feeling silly, but also relieved. "Sorry, bunny," she murmured. "Go back to your dinner."

"I guess your uncle Xenos's news has us all on edge," Ollie said. "But to be on the safe side, Beatrice, don't go anywhere by yourself. One of us should be with you all the time till Miranda's found."

Beatrice knew that Ollie meant well, but she had an independent streak that made her balk at being told what to do. And she didn't much like the suggestion that she needed Ollie—or anyone else, for that matter—to protect her.

"That's okay," Beatrice replied lightly, smiling so that Ollie's feelings wouldn't be hurt. "I can take care of myself."

Ollie got the message and, wisely, said no more.

That night, Beatrice tossed and turned, unable to sleep. Every creak in the old house made her pause mid-breath and listen intently. She told herself that she was being foolish, that she would laugh in the morning when sunlight flooded her room and erased the fears that only surface at night. But lying there alone in the dark, Beatrice fully expected to hear footsteps in the hall at any moment, then to see her bedroom door open slowly. And standing there, bathed in moonlight, would be Miranda Pengilly.

Beatrice reached out to stroke Cayenne, who was sleeping soundly beside her. The warm presence of the cat was comforting. Beatrice yawned, thinking that maybe she would finally be able to sleep. But her eyes were scarcely closed when she heard a crash somewhere in the house. The unexpected sound ran along the nerves of her body like an electric shock.

Beatrice sat straight up. Her heart was pounding hard against her ribs. She listened for a long time, as did Cayenne, who was now sitting rigidly at the foot of the bed, staring at the closed door. Beatrice knew that she would never be able to sleep if she didn't investigate the noise.

"I think it came from downstairs," she said softly to the cat. "Let's go see."

Beatrice crawled out of bed and shoved her feet into fuzzy green dragon slippers. She opened the bedroom door and stood very still in the darkness, listening, but the old house was silent except for the wheezing of an air conditioner that was on its last leg.

Beatrice stepped out into the hall. She felt the stirring of cool air on her bare ankles. Then something brushed against the hem of her long nightgown. A scream rose in Beatrice's throat—and she just managed to choke it off when she saw the shadow of a cat drifting past her toward the stairs.

"Cayenne, don't *do* that!" Beatrice hissed under her breath.

She took a few steps down the hall and stood for a moment outside her parents' bedroom. The door was opened slightly, and she could hear her mother's gentle breathing, as well as the louder snorts and smacks of her sleeping father. So it hadn't been either of her parents moving around downstairs.

Light from the moon spilled through the window onto the landing, guiding Beatrice down the staircase. Cayenne moved silently beside her, but Beatrice's weight caused each step to squeak or groan under her feet. She was relieved when they finally reached the downstairs hall.

Beatrice was peering into the dark living room when she heard another noise—like something heavy being knocked over—and she was pretty sure the sound had come from the cellar.

Beatrice tiptoed to the door beneath the stairs and grabbed hold of the knob. Then she hesitated. She had never liked going down to the cellar. It was dark and creepy, even in daylight. *And what if Miranda's down there waiting for me?* she thought. Her cousin's spellwork was no better than her own, but Miranda might be carrying a weapon. Beatrice imagined Miranda lurking in the dark with a baseball bat. Or a knife.

"Don't be ridiculous," Beatrice muttered to herself. "You've let your imagination run wild, and you're giving yourself the heebie-jeebies. Nobody's down there."

But *someone* had made that noise.

Cayenne looked up at her mistress and meowed sharply.

"*All right,*" Beatrice grumbled. "Why don't you go first?"

She turned the knob slowly. The door opened, with only a whisper of resistance as it brushed across the hardwood floor. Beatrice took a step forward and found herself peering down into total darkness. Stale air and dampness filled her nostrils.

Nasty, Beatrice thought. *Nasty and creepy.* But she took a deep breath to steady herself and began to feel along the wall inside the stairwell for the light switch. She flipped it on, and nothing happened.

Great! The bulb was probably burned out. Or someone could have *taken* it out. Beatrice thought about running back upstairs to wake her parents. Then she remembered that her father always kept a flashlight on the shelf above the light switch.

Beatrice's fingers found the shelf and crept along it, identifying all sorts of odds and ends, from gardening gloves to balls of twine—until she finally located the flashlight. Before she lost her nerve, Beatrice switched it on. The black stairwell was suddenly filled with brilliant light, and Beatrice was momentarily blinded. She couldn't hear anything, but she had a strong sense that someone—or *something*—was waiting at the bottom of the stairs.

Beatrice blinked rapidly, trying to adjust to the brightness. She realized that her eyes were adapting when she saw a dark blur dash past her down the narrow steps.

"Cayenne!" Beatrice called out in alarm, forgetting to be guarded in her fear for the cat's safety. And then, throwing caution to the wind, Beatrice started down the stairs.

The beam of the flashlight bounced erratically across the plank steps and rough plaster walls of the stairwell as Beatrice hurried after her cat. Cayenne reached the bottom of the staircase and disappeared around the corner. Close on the cat's tail, Beatrice came to the last step and stopped. She directed the flashlight beam into nearby nooks and crannies, looking for Cayenne and whoever was hiding in the cluttered cellar. The light danced across stacks of suitcases, old wing-back chairs with the stuffing coming out, a dragon kite, and Beatrice's first Wee Witch cauldron. Then it landed on the shallow window above the washing machine. Beatrice's heart plunged to the pit of her stomach when she saw it. Because the window was open!

Beatrice stood frozen, trying to quell the panic building up inside her. She knew her father kept the window closed, but the lock had been broken for years. It would have been easy for someone to open it from the outside, slide through, and then drop to the top of the washing machine.

Turning slowly, Beatrice watched for any movement. That's when the flashlight's beam caught the glow of two eyes staring out from behind a stack of boxes.

Beatrice's scream bounced off the rafters and echoed through the cellar. In an instant, Cayenne had whizzed past and was flying up the stairs. Beatrice whipped around to follow the cat, but her legs were trembling and she was only halfway up the staircase when she tripped. The flashlight fell from her hand and clattered down the steps to the concrete floor below.

She was struggling to her feet when she felt the grip of a hand on her shoulder. In a burst of desperation, Beatrice spun around and pushed as hard as she could at the body looming over her. It was too dark to see a face, but the shadow on the wall appeared enormous. A dozen terrifying thoughts swirled in Beatrice's head as she prepared to strike out again. But then she realized that the figure was teetering precariously on one of the narrow steps, and suddenly it went tumbling down the stairs and crashed, apparently lifeless, to the cellar floor.

Beatrice was too stunned to move. She was still crouching on the stairs when she heard footsteps above her head, and then her father's voice calling down to her, "Beatrice, is that you? Are you all right?"

"The light doesn't work," Mrs. Bailey said, sounding frantic.

"And the flashlight's gone," Mr. Bailey added. "Turn on the hall light."

As the cellar stairwell filled with light from the hall above, Cayenne came rushing down the steps to Beatrice.

"There she is," Mrs. Bailey said as she followed behind the cat. "Thank goodness!"

Then Mr. and Mrs. Bailey were kneeling on the step above Beatrice, hugging her while a distraught Cayenne rubbed against Beatrice's legs.

"Cayenne woke us," Mr. Bailey said. "She screamed her head off till we followed her. But what are you doing here in the middle of the night, Beatrice?"

Beatrice hadn't taken her eyes off the figure that lay crumpled in the shadows at the bottom of the stairs. Now she pointed and said in a shaky voice, "Someone broke into the cellar."

"Is it Miranda?" Mr. Bailey asked sharply.

But before Beatrice could answer, the intruder moaned and then rolled over, directly into the beam of the discarded flashlight.

"Oh, my gosh," Beatrice whispered.

Mrs. Bailey gasped, and then she exclaimed, "It's Ollie!"

"But what's he doing in our cellar?" Mr. Bailey asked in bewilderment.

Ollie moaned again, and Beatrice hurried down the steps to him.

"Ollie, speak to me!" she shouted, worry making the words come out more harshly than she intended. "Are you all right?"

He turned his head toward her and opened his eyes. "I think I'll live," he answered faintly, and managed a crooked smile.

Now Mrs. Bailey was bending over him, "Ollie, what in the world happened? Is anything broken?"

After moving his arms and legs and finding that they all still worked, Ollie sat up with Beatrice's help.

"I'm okay," he said, touching a lump on his forehead and grimacing. "Just a little headache."

"Do you realize that you scared me half to death clunking around down here?" Beatrice asked him, feeling both relieved and exasperated. "What were you doing, anyhow?"

"Guarding the house," he replied weakly. "I thought Miranda might show up."

"Well," Mr. Bailey said, "that was very thoughtful. Wasn't it, Beatrice?"

It was, but Beatrice was still put out. "Yeah, thoughtful," she said, frowning at Ollie. "But couldn't you have told me you were going to spend the night in our cellar?"

Ollie shrugged. "You don't want to believe that Miranda would hurt you," he said, "and you didn't like the idea of anyone protecting you. I figured you'd just tell me to go home."

Mrs. Bailey squeezed Ollie's shoulder. "You know Beatrice pretty well, don't you, dear?"

Beatrice's annoyance was fading, and she noticed that the lump over Ollie's eye was beginning to swell.

"I didn't mean to push you down the stairs," she said. "Let's go put some ice on that goose egg."

"And I'll fix you a cup of cat's purr tea for your headache," Mrs. Bailey added.

"With honey?" Ollie asked.

"Lots," Mrs. Bailey answered.

As Mr. Bailey and Beatrice helped Ollie to his feet, something fell from his hand. Beatrice stooped to pick it up, and her eyes opened wide when she saw what she was holding. It was a silver charm in the shape of a pentagram, with what appeared to be a tiny ruby in the center. Beatrice was thinking that it didn't belong to her or to her mother when she remembered something. The first time she had ever seen Miranda, her cousin had been wearing several long chains adorned with silver and ruby charms.

Beatrice's hand trembled as she stared at the penta-gram nestled in her palm. How could it have gotten here? *Unless . . .*

"Ollie," Beatrice said urgently, holding the charm out to him, "where did you find this?"

"On the washing machine. I stepped on it when I came in through the window."

"Was the window closed when you got here?"

"No, it was open. And that surprised me," Ollie admitted. "Shouldn't you keep it shut?"

"We do," Mr. Bailey said. "And I've been meaning to replace that broken lock."

But Beatrice was no longer listening. She realized now that her fears hadn't been ridiculous at all. Miranda had been here. Might *still* be here. Watching.

Beatrice studied all weekend. But it was impossible to keep her mind on schoolwork when every time a branch scraped against the house she was sure it was Miranda Pengilly trying to break in. Even so, Beatrice thought she did pretty well on most of her exams. Except for history, and maybe Spanish.

At noon on Friday, the last day of school before sum-mer vacation started, Beatrice and Teddy walked to the bul-letin board where final grades were posted. A noisy, jostling crowd had gathered, but Beatrice and Teddy managed to squeeze up to the front. Beatrice's tension began to ease as she scanned the sheets for each of her classes. A in English, B in science, B in phys. ed., A in art—and Beatrice actually smiled when she saw the C in Spanish. Then her eyes darted to her grade in American history. For a moment, she couldn't believe it. But there it was in black and white. The letter opposite her student number was an F.

Beatrice felt dazed. She had never failed a subject in her life.

"So how did you do?" Teddy asked. Then, seeing her friend's stunned face, she took Beatrice by the arm and pulled her through the crowd toward the door.

They met Cyrus as they were leaving the building.

"I got a D in math," he said happily.

"I know you'll want to celebrate *that*," Teddy said dryly.

Cyrus shrugged, grinning. "Okay, so I won't be on the honor roll with the brilliant Teddy Berry. But *who cares?* I passed, didn't I?"

Teddy glanced at Beatrice.

"It's all right, Teddy," Beatrice said, then added for Cyrus's benefit, "I failed history, so I guess I'll be going to summer school."

"*No way!*" Teddy exclaimed. "If you're in summer school, none of us will be able to go to the Witches'—"

Beatrice realized what she was going to say just as two boys passed by, staring curiously at the overwrought Teddy.

"*The Wind and the Willows,*" Beatrice said in a voice loud enough to drown out Teddy's. "That was one of *my* favorite books, too."

"Right," Teddy mumbled, and didn't speak again until they were a block away from school and no one else was around. Then she turned to Beatrice and said firmly, "I mean it, you can't go to summer school. You'll just have to take history over next year."

"They won't *let* you take seventh- and eighth-grade history at the same time," Beatrice answered, her tone despondent. "Mom and Dad are going to be so disappointed. I told them I wouldn't let our trips to the Sphere interfere with schoolwork."

"You've had a lot to deal with," Teddy replied. "What I think we should do," she went on doggedly, "is go by and get Ollie. He's good at talking reasonably to adults. Then we'll all discuss this with your parents. Don't they come home for lunch?"

"They do," Beatrice said apathetically, "but what's to talk about?"

"An alternative to summer school," Teddy retorted.

Ten minutes later, the four friends walked into Beatrice's kitchen, where Mr. and Mrs. Bailey were just sitting down to eat.

Mrs. Bailey took one look at her daughter's strained face and asked, "What's happened?"

Oddly enough, Beatrice's parents appeared relieved when she told them about her history grade.

"Oh, is that all?" Mr. Bailey responded.

"I thought you were going to tell us something awful," Mrs. Bailey said.

"Something threatening," Beatrice's father added. "But failing history isn't so bad."

"You can take it over in summer school," Mrs. Bailey said.

Teddy sprang to attention. "But if Beatrice has to go to summer school, our trip to the Sphere is out. Isn't there some other way to handle this?"

Beatrice blew her bangs aside and, looking very serious, said to her parents, "You know I don't mind if they classify me Everyday, but I do mind that I've let Teddy, Ollie, and Cyrus down. Not to mention Bromwich and his daughters. Can't I do something besides go to summer school?"

Mr. and Mrs. Bailey exchanged a look.

Then Mrs. Bailey turned back to Beatrice and said, "Why don't I call your guidance counselor and see what she recommends?"

"Tell her that Beatrice has promised to help some out-of-town relatives this summer," Mr. Bailey said to his wife, "and we think she should keep her word."

Beatrice caught her breath, thinking that she had the most wonderful parents in the world. "Do you suppose they might let me retake the exam sometime later in the summer?"

"We'll see," her mother said, and picked up the phone.

A few minutes later, Mrs. Bailey hung up and looked at Beatrice. "I guess you heard my questions about tutoring."

Beatrice nodded. "It sounded like Miss Badger had an idea," she said, waiting eagerly for her mother to announce a new plan.

But the reassuring smile that Beatrice had expected didn't materialize on Nina Bailey's face.

"Sweetheart," Mrs. Bailey said gently, and with that one word, Beatrice knew the worst, "Miss Badger said that you can retake the exam, but she thinks you're too far behind to do it on your own. That's why we were discussing a tutor."

"Okay, I'll get a tutor," Beatrice said quickly, ready to agree to anything. "Can she recommend someone?"

"She can," Mrs. Bailey replied. "But whether you go to summer school or have a tutor help you prepare for the exam, you'll still have to be here this summer to study. I'm sorry, Beatrice, but you need two history courses to graduate from middle school."

"She doesn't *have* to graduate," Teddy burst out. "When they make her Classical, she can go to a witch academy in the Sphere. *They* won't care about her mortal school record."

"I understand how important this trip is to you, Teddy," Mrs. Bailey said, "but we don't know how things are going to turn out. So for the time being, we have to assume that Beatrice will continue to go to school here."

The stricken look on Teddy's face made Beatrice feel terrible. "I really goofed up," she said miserably. "I'm *so* sorry, you guys."

"It's been a hard year for you," Ollie said, trying to hide his own disappointment. "We should have helped you more. It's as much our fault as it is yours."

That's when Beatrice did something that she never, ever did. She burst into tears.

3

Witches' Circle

That night, Beatrice and her friends stood around a small bonfire in Beatrice's backyard. To cheer them up, Beatrice's parents had suggested an impromptu wiener roast to celebrate the end of school. None of the four was in the mood for a celebration; but to avoid hurting Mr. and Mrs. Bailey's feelings, they had summoned up their party smiles and tried to throw themselves into the festivities. But now that the grown-ups had gone inside, there was no need to fake it.

"Does anyone want another marshmallow?" Cyrus asked listlessly.

"No, thanks," Beatrice said, "I have one." She watched morosely as the blackened marshmallow sagged on the end of the stick she was holding and then fell into the fire with a hiss.

Cyrus sighed and pitched his entire stick into the blaze, while Teddy sat down heavily in a lawn chair, narrowly missing a napping Cayenne, and stared bleakly into the dancing flames. Ollie was the only one who seemed able to muster any energy and made himself useful by picking up discarded paper plates and stuffing them into a trash bag.

"I should probably be going home," Cyrus said. "What time is it?"

Ollie squinted at his watch in the dim firelight. "Almost midnight. I guess I'd better be leaving, too."

About that time, Mr. and Mrs. Bailey came outside. When Beatrice saw that her mother was carrying a plate of brownies, she stifled a groan. She didn't think she could pretend all over again to be having a good time.

And then, as if the day hadn't been depressing enough, Beatrice saw a large ball of light drifting over the blackberry bushes toward them.

"Oh, no," she muttered.

The others followed her gaze. When Mrs. Bailey saw the glowing orb floating in their direction, she glanced anxiously at Beatrice.

"I should have sent a message to Aura and told her not to come," Mrs. Bailey whispered to her husband.

But it was too late now. The ball of light exploded, and the backyard was suddenly filled with a shower of falling stars and ribbons of fire. A startled Cayenne leaped to Beatrice's shoulder and glared at the unexpected fireworks display.

At any other time, Beatrice's first thought would have been to wonder if their mortal neighbors were noticing what was going on in the Baileys' backyard. But tonight she didn't care. Let them call the police. So what if they finally had proof that Beatrice and her parents were witches? What could they do about it, anyway, except treat the Baileys like outcasts? Which they already did!

Beatrice squared her shoulders and blew her bangs out of her eyes, preparing to face the thirteen members of the

Witches' Executive Committee. But then she did a double take—because standing in a meager semicircle on the other side of the bonfire were only three witches: Aura Featherstone, Leopold Meadowmouse, and Beatrice's witch adviser, Peregrine. Beatrice stared at them in confusion. Always before, the whole committee had come to announce her return to the Witches' Sphere, led by the director of the Witches' Institute, Dr. Thaddeus Thigpin. *Do they already know I won't be going to the Sphere?* Beatrice wondered. But if so, what were these three doing here?

With Cayenne still balanced on her shoulder, Beatrice walked around the fire toward the visiting witches, and her parents and friends followed. Beatrice's questioning eyes sought out Dr. Featherstone, who had always been Beatrice's staunchest ally on the committee.

Aura Featherstone was tall and uncommonly attractive, with auburn hair spilling across the shoulders of her sapphire-blue robes. The thirty-something witch exuded self-confidence and tended to be rather imposing, but the smile she gave Beatrice was warm.

"Merry meet," Dr. Featherstone said, her eyes moving from Beatrice to include the others. "I suppose you're wondering why there are only three of us here tonight."

"Let me tell her," Dr. Meadowmouse said eagerly.

Dressed in saffron-yellow robes, Leopold Meadowmouse had a long, genial face, which reminded Beatrice of a bloodhound, and a cap of brown hair that stood out from his head like a toadstool. Despite her low spirits, Beatrice couldn't help but smile at the kindly witch's enthusiasm.

When Dr. Featherstone nodded, Dr. Meadowmouse turned happily to Beatrice and said, "Thaddeus—that is,

Dr. Thigpin—has a little head cold. It's nothing serious, but the doctor suggested no travel for a few days, and the other committee members rarely go anywhere unless the director is along, so—" Dr. Meadowmouse shrugged and smiled more brightly—"Dr. Featherstone, Peregrine, and I have come to tell you that it's time for you to return to the Witches' Sphere."

Then he waited for the predictable reactions. Teddy and Cyrus could always be counted on to light up like search beacons, and even sensible Ollie would grin in anticipation. Of course, it was understood that Beatrice had mixed feelings about the test, but they had come to expect a torrent of questions from her regarding the obstacles they would face on their journey. So it was disconcerting for the committee members when Dr. Meadowmouse's announcement was met with blank stares. Then Teddy's shoulders slumped and her chin dropped to her chest, and the newly arrived witches knew that something was wrong.

Shy little Peregrine, whose slight four-foot frame was swallowed up by brown robes a size too large, had been partially hidden behind Dr. Featherstone. Now he stepped out. His large ears protruding through toast-colored hair gave him the appearance of an inquisitive bat as he peered inquiringly at Beatrice.

"Is there something we should know?" Peregrine asked softly.

Eight pairs of surprised eyes turned toward the little witch. He rarely spoke up at committee gatherings, but Beatrice realized that his concern for her was greater than his reluctance to call attention to himself, and she felt even more miserable and ashamed.

"Actually, there is something I need to tell you," Beatrice said in a small voice. "I can't go to the Witches' Sphere this time. I—failed my American history exam, so I have to be tutored and retake the exam."

The corners of Peregrine's small mouth drooped, and Dr. Meadowmouse murmured, "Oh, dear." But Dr. Featherstone seemed unaffected by Beatrice's news.

"Witches don't need American history," she said crisply. "They don't even teach that at the witch academies."

Teddy's eyes darted hopefully to Beatrice.

"But Beatrice goes to school here," Mrs. Bailey pointed out. And before Dr. Featherstone could assert her opinion again, Nina Bailey continued firmly, "We don't know if Beatrice will end up in the Witches' Sphere or if she'll stay in the mortal world. So for the time being, she has to prepare herself to live here—which includes passing all her subjects in a mortal school."

Aura Featherstone, who wasn't accustomed to being lectured, frowned at her old friend. Nina Bailey frowned right back. Then Dr. Featherstone opened her mouth to speak, but this time it was Dr. Meadowmouse who cut her off.

"She has a point, Aura," he said thoughtfully. "Beatrice can choose to live in the Sphere regardless of her classification, but she might be less inclined to leave her life here if she's classified Everyday."

"Blesséd be!" Dr. Featherstone's words came out as a small explosion. "Beatrice has already broken three parts of Dally Rumpe's spell. If that doesn't qualify her for a Classical classification, I don't know what does!"

Dr. Meadowmouse glanced uncomfortably at Beatrice and said to his colleague in a stage whisper, "Be that as it may, Aura, the full committee will have to vote on it after the test is completed. And Beatrice could still decide to live in the mortal world. It's her decision, after all."

Dr. Featherstone gave him a get-serious look, and then her brow furrowed as she paused to rethink the situation. Suddenly, a triumphant smile appeared on her lips.

"I have the perfect solution," Dr. Featherstone said with a hint of smugness. "Beatrice, you can study for this ridiculous exam and still go to the Sphere."

Beatrice's heart began to beat faster, but she was afraid to hope too much until she heard what Dr. Featherstone had to say. Teddy, on the other hand, was looking at Dr. Featherstone as if the older witch had just rescued her from drowning.

"How can she do that?" Mrs. Bailey asked doubtfully.

"By taking a tutor with her," Dr. Featherstone declared.

"But mortals aren't allowed in the Sphere," Mrs. Bailey reminded her.

"Who says that Beatrice's tutor has to be mortal?" Dr. Featherstone demanded. "There's a bright young witch working as an intern in my office this summer who would be the ideal tutor for Beatrice. His name is Ira Skelly, and he's doing graduate work at Witch U. I'm sure he'd prefer a vacation out west to running errands for me."

Mrs. Bailey was openly skeptical. "But what does someone from the Witches' Sphere know about American history?"

"It so happens, Nina, that Ira was born in the mortal world," Dr. Featherstone informed her. "His parents were

Reform, but they moved back to the Sphere when Ira was a teenager. He had *years* of mortal history crammed into his head before he escaped their brainwashing."

In the dying firelight, Beatrice saw her mother's eyes flash, but Dr. Meadowmouse stepped in adroitly. "Aura, perhaps you could summon Ira here, so that Mr. and Mrs. Bailey can meet him," he said.

"That's an excellent idea," Dr. Featherstone replied. "But before we do that, I suggest we go inside so that we'll have access to *The Bailiwick Family History*. These young witches are probably anxious to hear about their trip."

Beatrice was very nearly smiling as they all trooped into the house. Ollie and Cyrus were grinning, and Teddy practically danced down the hall to the living room. Aura Featherstone was obviously pleased with herself, and Dr. Meadowmouse and Peregrine seemed relieved that a solution had been found to Beatrice's problem. Only Mr. and Mrs. Bailey appeared uncertain.

Dr. Meadowmouse went straight to Mr. Bailey's desk. *The Bailiwick Family History* floated up into the air and landed in his hands.

Cayenne's body tensed on Beatrice's shoulder as the cat prepared to leap on any black beetles that happened to appear.

"I do love this history," Dr. Meadowmouse said, flipping through the brittle pages with satisfaction. Then he bent closer to read a passage. "How interesting. The entry has been updated, and now it tells us that Bromwich and Dally Rumpe are brothers."

"I know," Beatrice said hesitantly, not wanting to steal his thunder. "We've read that part."

"You have?" Dr. Meadowmouse didn't appear at all troubled by this admission. "And have you read about Blood Mountain, too?"

"Not much," Ollie answered. "We found out it's in the desert."

"But we didn't get to the part about the dangers we'll face," Teddy told him, her dark eyes sparkling with anticipation.

"All right then," Dr. Meadowmouse said briskly as he peered at the page in front of him. "Bromwich's fourth daughter, Morven, is held captive by Dally Rumpe on the top of Blood Mountain, which has the highest peaks in the region. Beatrice, you and your friends must climb the mountain, find Morven, and repeat the counterspell in her presence."

"There has to be more to it than just climbing a mountain," Beatrice said warily.

"Of course," Dr. Meadowmouse replied. "Blood Mountain is guarded by Ghumbabas."

"Twenty-foot giants," Dr. Featherstone responded to Beatrice's blank look. "They're an ancient race, known for their vicious temperament and grotesque appearance. Oh, and they never take baths."

"And circling the top of Blood Mountain," Dr. Meadowmouse went on, "are enormous birds of prey that swoop down on anyone who sets foot on the mountain. They grab intruders with their claws and drop them to the rocks below."

Beatrice sighed. "Okay, what else?"

"It says here," Dr. Meadowmouse murmured, frowning as he studied a passage in the book, "that the mountain is covered with deadly snakes and black widow spiders. And here's an interesting fact," he added. "Dally Rumpe's face has been carved into the side of the mountain. The sculpture is more than forty feet tall."

"Like Mount Rushmore!" Cyrus exclaimed. Then he saw Teddy rolling her eyes. "Well, *sort* of like Mount Rushmore," he muttered.

"What about the monster that guards Morven?" Dr. Featherstone asked.

"His name is Drude," Dr. Meadowmouse answered, "and he's an especially large and loathsome bird of prey, more savage than all the others put together. They say you can smell his horrible odor a mile away."

Teddy grimaced. "Filthy giants and a smelly bird of prey. I guess we'd better pack lots of deodorizer."

"And don't forget the snakebite antidote," Beatrice said grimly.

Mrs. Bailey was extremely pale. "Beatrice," she said faintly, "I'm still not convinced that this witch tutor is a good idea. And as for the snakes and giants . . ." Her voice trailed off.

"Nina," Dr. Featherstone said gently, "I know that you worry about Beatrice, but she's come back safe and sound from every trip, hasn't she? And freeing Bromwich and his daughters is, after all, her destiny. It was determined that she would do this long before we ever thought of testing her."

"From the moment she was born," Teddy pointed out.

Dr. Featherstone was studying Mrs. Bailey's face intently. "It seems to me," she said, "that some kind of magic is at work here that we don't understand. It appears to keep Beatrice safe."

"It *is* remarkable that she's been able to win out over Dally Rumpe," Dr. Meadowmouse agreed. He didn't add what they all were thinking: *And her just a simple Reform witch with no apparent talent for magic.*

Mrs. Bailey frowned. "I still don't like it," she said, and turned pleading eyes to her daughter. "Beatrice, you've already done so much. Why can't you let the next Bailiwick witch do the rest?"

"I don't want to worry you, Mom," Beatrice said quietly, "but I have to do this."

Mrs. Bailey's face reflected her frustration, but she spread her hands wide in a gesture of defeat. Then she gave Dr. Featherstone a penetrating look. "I'll be counting on that special magic, Aura—to bring my daughter back to me."

"Beatrice will be fine, Mrs. Bailey," Ollie said with conviction. "We watch out for one another."

Dr. Meadowmouse glanced at the clock on the mantle. "Shouldn't we be looking at the map?" he asked.

"Peregrine," Dr. Featherstone said, "do you have it?"

Peregrine withdrew a sheet of rolled-up parchment from inside his robes and spread it out on the desk. Everyone moved in for a closer look.

Beatrice was familiar with the Bailiwick map. Her eyes moved westward to the rugged peaks marked *Blood Mountain*, and she noticed that some smaller cliffs nearby had the words *Winged-Horse Mountain* printed above them. A cluster of buildings south of the mountains was identified as *Winged-Horse Ranch*.

"This is where you'll be staying," Dr. Featherstone said, pointing to the buildings. "It's a guest ranch, and I think you'll find it very comfortable."

"Interesting name," Beatrice said.

"The mountain and the ranch are named for Bromwich's favorite flying horse, Balto," Dr. Featherstone explained. "When Bromwich was imprisoned by Dally Rumpe, Balto managed to escape. Dally Rumpe can't stand knowing that there's something of Bromwich's that he doesn't possess, so he's been trying to catch Balto for two hundred years. But the horse has become wild and won't let anyone come near him."

"They say that Balto sometimes lands on top of Winged-Horse Mountain and paws the earth to create thunder and lightning," Dr. Meadowmouse said. "He's become a symbol of strength and freedom to the witches who live there."

"You'll see him for yourself on Monday," Dr. Featherstone said to Beatrice. "That's when you leave for Blood Mountain. And, of course, Peregrine will accompany you."

Teddy nudged Beatrice. "Tell them about Miranda," she said, her expression grim, as it always was when she mentioned Miranda Pengilly's name.

"Oh, yes," Dr. Featherstone said. "I meant to talk to you about your cousin, Beatrice. You've heard that she ran away from The Rightpath School?"

Beatrice nodded. "She came to our house."

Dr. Featherstone's eyebrows lifted. "You've seen her?"

"No, but she was here," Beatrice replied, and withdrew the silver and ruby pentagram from her shorts pocket. "She left this."

Dr. Featherstone looked closely at the charm. "A Bailiwick ruby," she murmured. Seeing the questions in

Beatrice's face, she added, "Bromwich selected the ruby to be the Bailiwick stone, perhaps because it symbolizes love and good deeds."

"It didn't hurt that he had his own ruby mines," Dr. Meadowmouse remarked.

"We forgot to mention that," Dr. Featherstone said to Beatrice. "The mines are located within Blood Mountain. Some of the most perfect rubies in the Witches' Sphere have come from there." She gestured toward the charm in Beatrice's hand. "A ruby this small isn't worth much, but I would guess that it came from the Bailiwick mines. Miranda's mother, Willow, used to wear silver and ruby charms like this one."

"Even if the ruby isn't valuable," Beatrice said, studying the pentagram, "as the Bailiwick stone, it would mean a lot to Miranda. Her name might be Pengilly, but as far as she's concerned, she's a Bailiwick."

"The point is," Teddy said impatiently, "Miranda almost killed us—*several times*—and now she's back. Can't you send out people to find her?" she demanded, staring hard at Dr. Featherstone.

"The authorities are looking for her," the older witch replied calmly, "but I don't think Miranda's after you. She probably just wanted to get away from that school. It has very strict rules, and Miranda was never fond of being told what to do."

Teddy was practically glaring now. "I don't think you realize just how dangerous Miranda Pengilly is," she said tightly. "The girl gave me witch fever. If she'd do that, she'd do *anything*."

"Although witch fever isn't fatal," Dr. Featherstone said with an amused gleam in her eyes, "I can see how your experience might make you distrust Miranda. But I doubt that she'll turn up at Winged-Horse Ranch. After all, the four of you can identify her, can't you?"

"If we see her first," Teddy said darkly.

Dr. Meadowmouse glanced at the mantle clock again. "We really should be wrapping this up, Aura," he said. "But weren't you going to bring Ira Skelly here so the Baileys can meet him?"

"If you insist," Dr. Featherstone muttered, and began to mumble something under her breath.

A minuscule ball of light appeared in front of her, then burst open with a feeble flash and a scattering of dust. Standing there was a frail-looking young witch in rumpled striped pajamas, his brown hair tousled and his dark eyes heavy with sleep. The man peered around in confusion at all the unfamiliar faces, then came to himself with a start.

"Sorry to wake you, Ira," Dr. Featherstone said. "Everyone, this is my summer intern, Ira Skelly. As I mentioned, he's a graduate student at Witch U, working on his doctorate in—witch psychology, isn't that right, Ira?"

Now wide awake, and apparently oblivious to the fact that he was being scrutinized in his jammies by a roomful of strangers, Ira drew himself up to his full, unimpressive height and said, "That's correct, Dr. Featherstone, with a concentration on the consequences of prolonged stress on the witch psyche. I intend to show a correlation between magical aptitude—and its effects on a witch's self-esteem—and his or her ability to cope with stress of long duration."

With these few words, Beatrice learned several things about the intern: that he was arrogant, that he was thrilled to have a chance to show off in front of his supervisor, and that his voice had a distinctly nasal quality that grated on her nerves. Beatrice sighed. Suddenly venomous snakes and stinky birds of prey seemed like the least of her problems.

Dr. Featherstone quickly introduced Ira to Mr. and Mrs. Bailey. "And this is Beatrice," she added, not seeming to notice Beatrice's glum expression. "She's in need of a tutor this summer, and that's why I called you here. I thought you'd be the perfect witch to help her with her studies in American history."

"Do you *know* anything about mortal history?" Mrs. Bailey asked.

Ira Skelly frowned. "When I was growing up in the mortal world, I learned more about their history than I care to recall," he replied stiffly.

Beatrice had a moment of hope. Maybe he wouldn't want the job and Dr. Featherstone would have to find someone else.

"Ira, you'll be traveling with Beatrice and her friends," Dr. Featherstone was saying. "They're leaving for Blood Mountain on Monday."

At the mention of Blood Mountain, Ira Skelly's whole demeanor changed. He was suddenly as excited as a werewolf pup.

"Did you say Blood Mountain?" he asked eagerly. "But that's perfect. Absolutely *perfect!* The witches in that part of the Sphere have been living with stress for more than two hundred years. The fieldwork I could do there would be *invaluable.*"

"But about your knowledge of American history," Mrs. Bailey persisted. "Are you quite sure you're qualified to tutor my daughter?"

The intern gave her an imperious smile. "Madam, when I was a senior at Witch U, I received the Hazel Twig Award for Scholarship," he informed her, puffing up with self-importance. "I might add that I'm the only witch to ever be given the award as an undergraduate. I *think* I should be able to instruct your child without any problem."

"Well then," Dr. Featherstone said cheerfully, ignoring Mrs. Bailey's disgusted expression, "shall we call it a night? Ira, come into the office early in the morning and we'll see about your travel orders."

Beatrice blew her bangs aside and caught Ollie's sympathetic eye. She tried to smile, but she knew that Ollie wasn't fooled. First Miranda, and now Ira Skelly. Beatrice had every reason to believe that this trip to the Witches' Sphere was going to be the toughest one yet.

4

Horse of a Different Color

On Monday morning, when Beatrice and her friends gathered on the Baileys' front porch, the sun was beginning to peek up over the trees and the air already felt hot and sticky. Peregrine was waiting for them on the front steps, Mrs. Bailey was handing out canteens and brown-bag lunches, and Mr. Bailey was lugging the last of their bulging backpacks out to the porch. The four friends were dressed in shorts and sturdy hiking shoes.

"Did everyone remember to bring sunblock and hats?" Teddy asked as she placed a very large, sombrero-style hat on her head.

Beatrice, Ollie, and Cyrus just stared at her, but the wide floppy brim hid most of her face from view.

"Do you really need to wear that thing now?" Beatrice asked while Teddy tightened the string under her chin. "You won't be able to see where you're going."

"It takes up too much room in my backpack," Teddy answered, throwing her head back so that she could look Beatrice in the eye. "And I had to leave some of my riding clothes at home as it was."

"*Riding clothes?*" Cyrus snickered.

Teddy gave Cyrus a cool, superior look, but with the brim of the sombrero falling over one eye, the effect was lost. "We *are* going to a western guest ranch," she informed him, "and I don't want to look like a greenhorn."

Cyrus squinted at the huge hat on her head. "Don't worry, Teddy," he said, trying to subdue an unruly grin that was forcing its way out. "You're gonna fit right in."

"Well," Beatrice said briskly, "I guess it's about time to get this show on the road."

Peregrine looked at her steadily. "Haven't you forgotten something?" he asked quietly.

"What?" Beatrice asked, nearly succeeding in making her face expressionless.

"*That,*" Peregrine replied, peering at the street.

Beatrice turned to look and saw Ira Skelly striding purposefully toward them. Beatrice's heart plunged to her feet. She had been hoping they could somehow avoid taking the tutor with them.

"Merry meet, everyone," Ira said as he came to a halt at the bottom of the steps.

Today, he was wearing neat khaki shorts and hiking shoes instead of rumpled pajamas. And with his hair combed, Beatrice realized that he wasn't bad looking, except that his small, penetrating eyes and sharp features reminded her of a weasel.

Ira lowered his backpack to the ground and they could see books and papers sticking out of the pockets.

"Didn't you bring any clothes?" Teddy asked him.

"There wasn't room for much after I packed my research materials," Ira replied curtly. "And this," he added, withdrawing an American history book that Beatrice recognized immediately. "I believe this is the text you've been using?"

Beatrice sighed. "That's the one."

"I thought we'd start going over some of the material on the trip," Ira said, withdrawing a thick sheaf of papers from the back of the book. "I've made up some questions to ask you," he added, peering down at the papers in his hand. *"What was the name of the first English settlement in the New World,"* he read, *"when was it founded, and by whom?"*

"It was—Jamestown," Beatrice said, stuttering a little because the tutor had caught her off guard.

Ira's black eyes bore into her face. "And the date?" he asked sharply. "This is very basic, Beatrice. Surely you know the founding date."

Beatrice was chewing nervously on her bottom lip, thinking, *I did know the date. I'm sure I knew it before the exam.* But as her tutor stared at her, seeming to grow more impatient by the second, any dates she had known slipped right out of her head.

Ira frowned. "It was May 19, 1607," he said sternly, and then muttered, "I can see I have my work cut out for me."

"This tutoring business can wait," Peregrine said, his tone unusually firm as he scowled at Ira Skelly. "You'll have plenty of time to quiz Beatrice once we reach Winged-Horse Ranch."

Beatrice flashed her witch adviser a grateful smile, and her friends were all grinning their approval. Ira Skelly, on the other hand, looked furious.

"So," Peregrine continued, ignoring the tutor as he tucked the lunch Mrs. Bailey had given him inside his robes, "are we ready to go?"

"Just about," Beatrice said.

She picked Cayenne up gently and placed her in a pocket of the backpack, so that only the cat's head was visible. Then Beatrice's parents were hugging Beatrice and her friends good-bye and admonishing them to be careful.

"Don't take any unnecessary risks!" Mrs. Bailey called out as the travelers started down the front steps. "And study hard, Beatrice."

"Watch out for Miranda!" Mr. Bailey shouted as the procession headed down the street.

At the first intersection, Peregrine turned right and entered the woods. They tramped through dense undergrowth until the trees began to thin out and finally emerged into a large meadow. On their last trip, a hot-air balloon had been waiting in the meadow to take them to Sea-Dragon Bay; but this time, there were six horses tethered in the center of the field.

"Wow!" Cyrus exclaimed, his blue eyes shining. "We're going on horseback?"

"This is great," Ollie said.

Beatrice noticed how the horses' coats gleamed in the early morning sun. One was black, one was the dark reddish color of autumn leaves, one was pale tan, two were dark brown, and—Beatrice blinked. Was the light playing tricks on her? Or could there really be a *purple* horse grazing contentedly with the others?

Teddy was staring with her mouth open. "Is that horse dark gray or is it . . . ?"

"Purple," Cyrus said firmly. "The horse is definitely purple!"

Then Beatrice noticed that there was something unusual about *all* the horses. Tucked against their sides, just in front of the saddles, were what appeared to be folded wings.

Beatrice peered closer at the animals. "Peregrine, do these horses have wings?" she asked.

"Of course," the witch adviser replied. "How else would they be able to fly?"

They walked across the field to the horses and Peregrine began to untie the reins. Teddy was given the black horse, Ollie the tan one, and Cyrus and Ira the brown ones. Peregrine held out the reins of the purple horse to Beatrice.

"How did I know?" Beatrice muttered, and was instantly sorry, because the purple horse turned its head to look at her with the largest, most sorrowful eyes Beatrice had ever seen.

"Her name is Plum," Peregrine said. Then he added in a whisper, "She's sensitive about her coloring, but she's the fastest horse at Winged-Horse Ranch."

"Hello, Plum," Beatrice said gently, stroking the mare's thick purplish mane. "I think your color is quite—*distinctive*. And your name is certainly appropriate."

Plum jerked her head and snorted loudly, spraying Beatrice's face with wetness. Cayenne, who had been peering out of the backpack over Beatrice's shoulder, also received a shower. The cat hissed and began to wipe a frenzied paw across her nose.

"*That* wasn't very nice," Beatrice said indignan?' the horse, and mopped at her own face.

"Have you all ridden before?" Peregrine asked.

Everyone answered that they had, except for Cyrus, who was staring up at the large brown mare beside him with sudden trepidation. "She's a lot bigger up close," he mumbled.

Ira was smirking at him. "I take it you've never been on a horse," he said.

"I have, too," Cyrus replied defensively. "We had pony rides at my fourth birthday party."

Ira's laugh came out as a rude bark, and he started to say something—but Peregrine cut him off.

"That's fine," Peregrine said to Cyrus. "Just grip the saddle with your knees and hold on tight to the horn. That's that thing on top of the saddle. Okay, everybody, mount up."

They all managed to hoist themselves into their saddles without too much trouble, although Cyrus's face went very pale when he looked down from his perch atop the large mare's back. Peregrine was busy leading the horses into a line and then snapping a long leather strap onto each of the bridles.

"What do we need that for?" Ollie asked the witch adviser.

"So we'll stay together," Peregrine said. "Once we're airborne, it would be easy for someone to lag behind and get lost."

"Airborne?" Cyrus repeated softly, and grabbed hold of the saddle horn so tightly his knuckles turned white.

Even though he was the smallest of all of them, Peregrine mounted the lead horse with surprising ease. Then peering around at his fellow travelers, he said with a crooked smile, "Is everybody ready?"

"Ready," came the unified response.

Plum was the last horse in line, directly behind Ollie's horse. As they started across the field toward the woods, Ollie looked over his shoulder at Beatrice and grinned. "Prepare for takeoff," he said cheerfully.

But instead of soaring into the air, the horses continued to canter across the grass until they entered the trees. Then they were forced to slow down as thick roots caught at their hooves and brambles snagged their manes and tails.

"I thought we were going to fly," Teddy said.

"Not while we're in the mortal world," Peregrine replied. "Can't you imagine the hysteria if some mortal looked up and saw a string of horses flying overhead?"

Beatrice laughed. In her mind, she could picture Amanda Bugg and Olivia Klink staring in astonishment at Beatrice astride a flying horse—and a purple one, at that.

As they made their way deeper into the woods, Beatrice noticed that it was becoming darker, as if the sun were covered by heavy clouds. Soon Ollie and his horse seemed to be swallowed up in blackness.

"We've entered The Borderlands," Peregrine called out, "the region between the mortal world and the Witches' Sphere. We'll be leaving the ground as soon as we're clear of the trees."

It wasn't long before Beatrice felt Plum rising beneath her. Then the horse sped up and turned sharply skyward, like an airplane leaving the runway. Beatrice felt her stomach lurch at the same time Cyrus cried out, "Couldn't we just *walk* to Blood Mountain?"

Before long, Plum finished her assent behind the other horses and Beatrice felt the horse begin to level off.

Beatrice let out the breath she had been holding and began to relax. Actually, it was kind of fun now that she wasn't afraid of sliding off the back and falling who knew how many feet to earth. With the cool wind whipping her hair into a tangle, Beatrice felt like she was sailing through the air on a glider.

As they flew on through the darkness, Beatrice realized that the air around them was growing warmer. Soon the wind in her face felt like the blast from a furnace, and it was hard for Beatrice to catch her breath. She leaned forward, using Plum's broad neck as a shield from the scalding wind. When she sat up again, Beatrice noticed that the darkness was starting to lift. They were entering the Witches' Sphere.

Gradually, the sky turned from charcoal to pale dove gray, and then to a sun-drenched blue that was so brilliant it brought tears to Beatrice's eyes. She blinked them away and squinted at the landscape below.

Desert sands spread out as far as she could see, broken only by an occasional giant cactus. It was a forbidding land, dry and alien, and yet beautiful in its own way.

The heat engulfed them and the sun beat down unmercifully on the top of Beatrice's head. She found herself envying Teddy and that ridiculous sombrero. Then she heard Peregrine calling out, "Hold on! We'll be landing in a minute."

As the horses made their descent, the air seemed to grow even hotter. Beatrice felt light-headed. She squeezed her eyes shut and held on for dear life to the saddle horn.

There was a jolt when Plum's hooves hit the ground and Beatrice was nearly thrown from the saddle. She opened her eyes, swaying a little as the heat rose up around her from the sand.

Ollie looked back at her, his face very pale. "Are you okay?" he asked.

Beatrice nodded, then stopped when her head began to spin. "I'm fine," she answered weakly.

"This sun is awful!" Teddy exclaimed. "We need to find shade."

Now Beatrice could see that all her companions appeared shaky.

"We'll stop up ahead," Peregrine told them, pointing to an enormous cactus.

The caravan of horses made its way slowly toward the cactus. When Beatrice felt the shade from one of its massive arms fall over her, she slid from the saddle and collapsed onto the sand. The others did the same. Too drained of energy to move, their bones turned to liquid, they lay there for several minutes without speaking. But Beatrice was thirsty, and finally, she managed to stagger to her feet and find the canteen in her saddlebag.

Water had never tasted so delicious! Beatrice gulped greedily, inspiring the others to reach for their own canteens. They poured water into a pail Peregrine had brought for the horses, and made a halfhearted attempt to eat the lunches Mrs. Bailey had prepared for them. But no one was especially hungry, even Cayenne, so the horses got most of the food.

While they rested, they stared intently at the two mountains in the distance. The closest one was the color of the desert, pale gold streaked with umber shadows.

"That's Winged-Horse Mountain," Peregrine said. "The ranch is just to the south, but you can't see it from here."

And just beyond, its jagged peaks rising even higher from the desert floor, was Blood Mountain. With its crimson sun shining overhead like an angry boil, the mountain was aptly named. It was the sickening color of dried blood.

Beatrice's heart began to beat faster as she stared at the rusty-red cliffs looming over the smaller mountain. She knew she was just imagining it, but it seemed that she could *smell* blood. Despite the heat, a chill crept down her spine.

"As you can see," Peregrine said, "Blood Mountain has its own sun. The rest of the desert becomes dark at night, but the red sun never sets."

Beatrice noticed a dozen or more black specks in the sky above Blood Mountain. "What are those tiny dots floating at the top of the mountain?" she asked.

"Birds of prey," Peregrine said solemnly, "and up close, they aren't so tiny. They're about the size of one of these horses."

This pronouncement served to silence everyone except Ira Skelly. The tutor had pulled Beatrice's history text from his backpack and was flipping through it. "No point in wasting all this time," he said, his self-righteous tone suggesting that they were a pretty shiftless lot. "And since Dr. Featherstone is paying me to tutor . . ."

He cut his eyes at Beatrice and she bristled.

"I hardly think this is the time or the place for a study session," she said hotly.

And as if to prove the point, the sand nearby shifted slightly and caught Beatrice's attention. She watched in horror as a large diamond-backed snake slithered toward them.

Beatrice grabbed for Cayenne and scrambled to her feet, pointing. Ollie gasped and Teddy screamed. Cyrus and Peregrine leaped up and made a panicked dash for cover behind the horses. Ira didn't understand what was happening and stared at them in astonishment. Then he saw something move at his feet and his eyes opened wide with terror.

"Get out of the way, you doofus!" Beatrice bellowed.

Ira didn't have to be told twice. He vaulted over the coiled body of the snake and threw himself onto the nearest horse, who happened to be Plum. The mare jerked her head around to glare at him and whinnied a sharp warning.

No one spoke until the snake had slithered away. Then Peregrine said in a quivering voice, "I think the sooner we get to the ranch, the better."

"I couldn't agree more," Teddy said curtly, and ran for her horse.

A half hour later, with Winged-Horse Mountain looming over them, they arrived at a cluster of sprawling adobe buildings that rested in the shadow of the mountain. Beyond the buildings, they could see horses in a large fenced paddock.

"Well," Peregrine said as they came to a halt at the wide front gates, "this is Winged-Horse Ranch."

"And *that*," Ollie said, staring up at the top of the mountain, "must be the winged horse."

Beatrice threw her head back to look and caught her breath sharply. A white horse with enormous feathered wings and a white mane and tail as fine as silk thread was flying above the mountain. So this was Balto. He was the most beautiful creature she had ever seen!

Beatrice blew her bangs aside and followed the stallion's movements with her eyes. His body was massive, and yet he seemed to glide as effortlessly as a sparrow.

Balto circled the mountain once again, flying lower this time, and then landed gently on the uppermost peak. He seemed to be looking directly at them. Beatrice had the feeling that the horse was not only aware of their respectful attention, but considered it his due.

While they watched, Balto lifted one powerful front leg and pawed the earth. With each strike of his hoof, there was a deep rumble of thunder. Then lightning flashed across the top of the mountain, and the horse raised his head to the sky and emitted a whinny that sounded like laughter.

Beatrice found herself laughing, as well. "What a gorgeous animal," she said.

"The only one of us still free," responded a deep voice.

Beatrice and her companions turned in the direction of the voice, their eyes scanning the few stunted trees and underbrush that grew at the base of the mountain. A figure in faded brown witches' robes was standing among the trees, watching them. He was holding an enormous hunter's bow and had a quiver of arrows slung over his shoulder. Then Beatrice noticed that he was leaning on a crudely made crutch, and although his face was concealed by the hood he wore, she had the impression that he was old and frail.

"Who are you?" Beatrice asked.

"My name is Orion," the man replied in that same deep voice.

Remembering her study of the constellations, Beatrice glanced at Ollie and said, "The hunter."

She had hoped to ask him more about himself and about the horse who had remained free. But when her eyes returned to the spot where Orion had been standing, he was gone.

5

Winged-Horse Ranch

They rode through the gates into the ranch yard. The main house was a two-story adobe faded to a pale pink by the sun. A shaded veranda encircled the building, and at the back, Beatrice caught sight of umbrella-topped tables and the sparkling chlorine-blue water of a swimming pool. In her current hot and gritty state, she looked longingly at the water and was tempted to kick off her hiking shoes and jump in without bothering to change her clothes. But the sounds of children laughing and shouting broke into her daydream, and she reluctantly looked away from the pool to the sandy field on the other side of the ranch house.

A large group of girls and boys was gathered on the field for archery practice. None appeared to be older than ten or eleven, and the art of hitting a bull's-eye with a bow and arrow was obviously something new to them. Arrows were flying everywhere, with very few coming anywhere near the targets.

"Those are the campers," Peregrine said, watching the young archers with interest. "Besides being a year-round guest ranch, this is also a summer camp. I came here when I was nine," the witch adviser added with a nostalgic sigh. "It was the best summer of my life."

Just then, something whizzed past Beatrice's head, so close she could feel the air stirring beside her right ear, and her eyes fell on an arrow that had struck the sand a few feet away. She stiffened, realizing that she had barely escaped becoming a human bull's-eye.

"Oh, my," Peregrine said, looking distressed. "That nearly hit you, didn't it?"

One of the campers came racing toward them, and then screeched to a halt when he saw the arrow sticking out of the ground. He was smaller than most of the others, with black curly hair and dark eyes. Beatrice watched his expression change from apprehension to dismay. It was obvious that he had shot the rogue arrow, but he appeared so horrified by what he had done, Beatrice didn't have the heart to chew him out.

Peregrine, on the other hand, didn't hesitate to speak up. "Do you know that you could have killed someone with that arrow?" he demanded, staring down hard at the boy from the back of his horse.

Beatrice had never known her bashful, kindhearted witch adviser to be so stern. Then she saw the worry in his eyes and realized that it was Peregrine's concern for her safety that had provoked the sharp response.

"I'm sorry!" the boy burst out, his voice shrill with anxiety. "I didn't mean to shoot it this way. Honest! It was an accident."

The young offender's dark eyes were now swimming with tears, and Peregrine's face softened.

"Well, no real harm done," the witch adviser said. "But be more careful in the future."

The boy nodded vigorously, sniffling as he blinked away tears.

Beatrice slid off Plum's back and walked over to the boy.

"What's your name?" she asked, thinking what a beautiful child he was, and already forgetting how frightened she had been.

The boy looked up at her from under thick black lashes that were wet and sticking together. "Kasper Cloud," he replied solemnly.

"I'm Beatrice Bailey," she said. "My friends and I will be staying at the ranch for a while."

"I know." Kasper regarded her steadily, his expression thoughtful. "There was an article in the paper that said you were coming here to try to break Dally Rumpe's spell on Blood Mountain."

This came as no surprise to Beatrice. In eight short months, she had gone from total obscurity to being the biggest news story in the Witches' Sphere. *Lowly Reform Witch Does the Impossible!* Beatrice sighed. What she wouldn't give to be a nobody again.

"I really am sorry," Kasper said, and added matter-of-factly, "I'm the worst archer at camp. Also the worst swimmer and the worst rider."

"I doubt that," Beatrice said hastily.

"But it's true," Kasper replied calmly. "I've been going to camp since I was four, and I'm ten now, so I should be getting better at this stuff."

Teddy had gotten off her horse and come to join them. "Isn't four awfully young for camp?" she asked Kasper.

"Probably," he agreed, "but Mom and Dad work all the time, so I'm a boarding student at the witch academy during the school year and they send me to different camps in the summer."

There was something wistful, yet resigned, in his voice that plucked at Beatrice's heart. "Do you enjoy going to camp?" she asked gently.

Kasper shrugged. "It's okay. And like Dad says, I'd be lonely at home by myself." Suddenly he looked intently at Beatrice. "My mom works at the Witches' Institute. She's a lawyer, and I heard her tell my dad that she stays really busy because of you."

Beatrice was taken aback. "*Me*? Why do *I* keep her busy?"

"Because every time you come to the Witches' Sphere, she has to research whether the things you do are legal or not. Like the time you became friends with that smuggler in Friar's Lantern, and then he smuggled your mother into the Sphere—after she'd been banished and wasn't supposed to ever come back." Kasper's dark eyes were sparkling now, and he very nearly smiled. "Mom told Dad that *that* was a legal nightmare."

Beatrice could feel her face turning pink.

"And then there was the time your witch adviser was accused of helping Dally Rumpe," Kasper went on doggedly, "and Mom was told that she would be defending him if the case ever went to trial."

"But I was exonerated!" Peregrine protested, beginning to tremble as he was reminded of the worst experience of his life.

Kasper shrugged again. "Mom had to prepare for the case, anyway," he said to Peregrine. "If you're ever in trouble again, you should call her. She's a very good lawyer."

"Bite your tongue," Peregrine muttered.

Beatrice was smiling now. She liked this forthright little witch, even if he *had* nearly turned her into a witch kebab.

"So does your father work at the Witches' Institute, too?" she asked.

"Uh-uh. He's the CEO of The Real Good Magic Company."

"I'll bet you get great birthday gifts," Beatrice guessed.

Kasper was finally grinning and looked like the ten-year-old boy he was instead of a somber old man. "That's true," he said cheerfully. "Thank goodness Dad brings my gifts home from work. If he left it up to Mom, I'd be getting sweaters and underwear."

"I hate to break up this *fascinating* conversation," Ira Skelly said loudly, clearly petulant, "but shouldn't we be going inside? Before our *brains melt?*"

Teddy scowled at him and Cyrus rolled his eyes. Everyone else ignored him.

"There's Joy," Kasper said suddenly as a pretty young woman came out of the main house and started toward them. "She runs the ranch for Mr. Griffin."

The woman had sun-streaked brown hair that fell to her shoulders, and Beatrice noticed that she was wearing a pair of scuffed cowboy boots under her blue robes.

"Merry meet and welcome," the woman said as she approached them, and then extended her hand to Beatrice. "I'm Joy Rowntree. And you must be Beatrice Bailey."

Beatrice introduced her companions and Joy smiled as she shook their hands. But watching her, Beatrice noticed that the smile didn't quite reach her gray eyes. Beatrice thought those beautiful eyes were the saddest she had ever seen.

"I'll show you to the stables," Joy said, "and one of the stable hands will take care of the horses."

They all started after her, including Kasper. Joy gave the boy a meaningful look. "Aren't you supposed to be at archery practice?"

"If you're smart, you'll keep me away from sharp objects," Kasper replied with a straight face, but his eyes were sparkling again. "In my hands, they could be lethal."

"Be that as it may," Joy responded, the smile warming her eyes this time, "your parents are paying a hefty sum for you to learn how to shoot a bow and arrow. So scoot!"

"She's a tyrant," Kasper informed Beatrice, and then took off at a gallop toward the archery field. "I'll see you later!" he called over his shoulder.

They had arrived at the stables, where several horses were already corralled in the paddock. A plump little man who was no more than two feet tall was pouring water into one of the horse troughs. He was wearing a red-checked shirt and his pant legs were stuffed into small red cowboy boots similar to Joy's. His very round belly was partially hidden by a white beard that fell nearly to his knees.

"Longfellow," Joy called out to the man, "come over and meet our guests."

"Not a brownie," Beatrice murmured. "And I don't think he's an elf . . ."

71

"Gnome, western variety," Joy informed her. "We don't have brownies and elves in this part of the Sphere."

"Thanks," Beatrice said. She always had trouble identifying unfamiliar magical creatures.

The gnome hurried over to where they stood, but seemed more interested in the horses than in Beatrice and her companions. In fact, he brushed right past Beatrice and made straight for Ollie's mare, where he began to examine one of the animal's forelegs.

"Did you notice any lameness after she landed?" the gnome asked, not looking up as his small hands moved slowly down the horse's leg.

"Uh—no—I don't think so," Ollie replied uncertainly. "Is something wrong with her?"

"She's prone to tendinitis," the gnome responded, "but that leg looks pretty good."

"*Longfellow*," Joy said, sounding a bit impatient, "you can see to the horses in a minute. I want to introduce our new guests."

Longfellow turned around, dusting his hands off and seeming to notice Beatrice and her companions for the first time.

"This is Longfellow, our best stable hand," Joy said to Beatrice.

"Longfellow like the poet?" Beatrice asked.

The gnome put his hand under his chin in a thoughtful pose and said, "Now there's a story—which I'll be glad to tell you when you have some time. But meanwhile, let's just say that my mother had a fondness for mortal writers and named her sons according to what she was reading when they were born. My brothers are Dickens, Chaucer, and O. Henry."

Beatrice grinned.

"Longfellow," Joy said, "this is Beatrice Bailey. Everyone in her party is to be given horses whenever they request them." She gave the gnome a penetrating look. "Your rule about letting the horses rest for *days* between rides doesn't apply to them."

Longfellow was frowning now and studying the toe of his boot. "You can't ride 'em to death and expect 'em to perform well," he muttered. Then he looked up and gave Joy a sly smile. "Does Mr. Griffin agree with giving the Bailey party special treatment?"

It was Joy's turn to frown. "That's none of your concern," she said crisply, and then glanced at Beatrice. "I'm sure you'd like to wash up and rest after your trip. I'll take you to your rooms."

When they came through the front door of the main house, they were greeted by deliciously cool air. Beatrice sighed with pleasure, and Teddy removed her sombrero for the first time that day.

They were in a large room that had a high ceiling and white plastered walls, with comfortable chairs and sofas arranged around a huge stone fireplace. Colorful rugs bearing designs of fierce birds and winged horses were scattered across the tiled floor.

A round little man with a white beard came toward them, and for a moment Beatrice thought that Longfellow had somehow managed to beat them inside, but then she noticed that the man's boots were black rather than red, and his beard only reached to the middle of his chest.

"Oh, there you are, Dickens," Joy said. "Will you take our guests' bags up to their rooms? Number three for the girls . . ." Then she paused, studying the four males. "We weren't expecting so many in your party, and we're booked to capacity. I'm afraid we only have two rooms available."

Obviously a witch who tried to keep her guests happy, Joy looked relieved when Peregrine said, "I won't be staying." But her relief was short-lived when Ira Skelly informed her that he would be needing a private room.

"We don't have a private room at the moment," Joy told him.

"That's all right," Ollie replied quickly. "Ira can bunk with Cyrus and me."

Joy flashed him a grateful smile. "It's a double room with twin beds, and I can have a cot moved in."

Ira's disgruntled expression made it clear that he was none too happy with these arrangements. "Well, you two can flip for the cot," he said sourly to Ollie.

Just then, a door behind the front desk opened and a middle-aged man stepped out. He was stocky and not much taller than Beatrice, with faded sandy hair and a weathered face that appeared to be set in a permanent frown. He stopped short when he saw Beatrice and her companions, and his blue eyes narrowed suspiciously.

"This is Seamus Griffin," Joy said, "the owner of Winged-Horse Ranch."

Under Seamus's unfriendly scrutiny, Beatrice's smile faded and the greeting she had been about to utter died on her lips.

Glancing from the man to Beatrice and back again, Ollie jumped in hastily. "It's great to be here, sir," he said, as if he didn't notice the ranch owner's scowl. "Thank you for having us."

"It wasn't *my* idea," Seamus said, staring fiercely at Beatrice. "In fact, I don't want you here at all!"

Beatrice blinked—she didn't know *how* to respond to this—and Joy hurried over to the man and placed a calming hand on his arm.

"Remember, Seamus," Joy said softly, "they're our guests."

"They have no business being here," he answered, his voice as steely as the blue eyes still boring into Beatrice's face. "That Aura Featherstone says I can't send you packing, but don't expect any help from me or my staff on this foolish mission of yours."

With that, he walked out from behind the desk and stalked through the front door without looking back.

Joy appeared embarrassed—*and troubled*, Beatrice thought. But the ranch manager produced a smile that was meant to be comforting and said lightly, "Don't take anything Seamus says personally. He just has a lot on his mind. Dickens, why don't you take our guests to their rooms? Number three for the ladies, and four for the gentlemen."

"I'll leave you now," Peregrine said to Beatrice. "I don't suppose you'll be getting any instructions from the Executive Committee," he added with a faint smile, "since you haven't been waiting for their directions lately. Just be careful, and I'll see you again once you've broken the spell on Blood Mountain."

And then he was gone. Vanished, just like that. But Beatrice wasn't surprised. She had gotten used to witches from the Institute popping in and out of her life with no warning.

As they followed Dickens up the stairs to the second floor, Beatrice said, "You're Longfellow's brother, aren't you?"

Dickens glanced at her over his shoulder and said cheerfully, "So you've met Longfellow, have you? He's my older brother—*much* older—but he doesn't like to be reminded of his age. Three hundred and forty seven his last birthday."

The gnome led them down the hall and opened the door to Room Three. Cayenne scrambled out of the backpack and ran inside.

"You gentlemen are across the hall," Dickens said.

Beatrice and Teddy followed Cayenne into a small, sparsely furnished room that would have looked at home in a bunkhouse. There were two narrow beds covered with brightly striped blankets, a pine chest of drawers, a writing table, and a straight-back chair. Through an open door, they could see a white-tiled bathroom.

Cayenne leaped to one of the beds and stretched.

Beatrice lay down beside the cat. "This feels good," she said wearily.

Teddy hoisted her backpack onto the other bed and started rifling through it. "I can't wait to take a shower. Do you mind if I go first?"

Beatrice closed her eyes and yawned. "I'm too tired to move right now, anyway," she answered. "I think I'll take a quick nap."

Teddy went to shut the door to the hall and slammed it into something solid. A frowning Ira Skelly stepped hastily into the room.

"Oh," Teddy said. "Sorry."

Ira rubbed his elbow and glowered at her. "You should be more careful," he snapped. Then he turned to Beatrice, who had started feeling a little nauseous at the sight of him.

He dropped the American history book onto the bed, barely missing Cayenne, who gave him a menacing look.

"Read Chapters One through Four," Ira said, his tone making it clear that this was an order, not a request, "and answer the questions at the back of each chapter. I'll expect to have them before dinner tomorrow evening."

Beatrice sat straight up, fully awake now. "*Four chapters?* But I can't possibly do all that in one day!" she protested.

"See if you can't change that negative attitude," Ira said curtly. "Oh, and I'll be grading your grammar and spelling, as well as the content of your answers."

With that, Ira left the room, slamming the door behind him.

Beatrice picked up the textbook and stared at it incredulously. "Four chapters," she muttered. "This guy is nuts!"

"It won't take that long," Teddy consoled her as she headed for the bathroom. "Why don't you start reading now?"

Beatrice put down the textbook with a grimace and turned to look out the window. There was Winged-Horse Mountain, and behind it, the jagged red peaks of Blood Mountain.

She stood up and walked over to the window for a better look. That's when she noticed the smoke. And the *flames!* Winged-Horse Mountain was on fire!

6

Wildfire

Beatrice cried out in alarm, and Teddy came barreling from the bathroom.

"What is it?" Teddy demanded, peering anxiously around the room.

"There's a fire on the mountain!" Beatrice exclaimed, already heading for the door.

They met Ollie, Cyrus, and Ira in the corridor.

"We heard you yell," Ollie said.

"Winged-Horse Mountain's on fire," Beatrice told him.

They raced down the stairs and out into the yard. Joy and Seamus were there, along with some of the campers and a group of adult witches that Beatrice assumed to be other guests and staff members. Then she saw at least two dozen gnomes starting up the side of Winged-Horse Mountain with buckets. Above them, dry brush crackled as it was engulfed in flames.

Beatrice stared in stunned silence as the gnomes scampered up the rugged cliffs, surprisingly fast for their size. When the first ones reached the burning brush, they emptied buckets of water on the wildfire, causing it to hiss and smoke.

"What happened?" Beatrice asked Joy.

"*Balto* happened," Joy replied, and Beatrice noticed that the woman didn't seem especially concerned.

Seeing Beatrice's perplexed expression, Joy laughed lightly. "Every time that horse paws the ground he causes thunder and lightning, and we usually end up with a lightning fire. But the gnomes have become pretty good at putting them out."

"Does Balto start fires on purpose?" Cyrus asked.

The smile faded from Joy's face, replaced by sadness. "He still misses Bromwich, even after all this time," she said quietly, "and his sorrow turns to anger. So," she added with a shrug, "he makes trouble."

"Look there," Ollie said suddenly, pointing to the base of the mountain. "Is that a miniature village?"

Beatrice peered in the direction of Ollie's finger and saw a cluster of tiny cottages nestled among the rocks and stunted trees. They weren't readily noticeable because they were made from the same pale stone as the mountain. Even their tiled roofs and small wooden doors were the color of desert sand.

Beatrice could see a group of female gnomes with their children gathered around the cottages, watching as the men braved the fire. The women were short and round like the men, but they wore long, full skirts and kerchiefs over their braided hair.

"There must be fifty or sixty gnomes here," Beatrice said in amazement. "Surely they don't all work at the ranch."

"Only Longfellow and Dickens," Joy replied, "and Longfellow's wife and daughters do our cleaning and laundry. The other gnome women care for their families and homes, while the men work in the mines."

"The ruby mines," Teddy said.

"That's right," Joy replied, her eyes still following the firefighters as they trekked up the cliff with more buckets. "That's what those tracks on Blood Mountain are for."

At the mention of ruby mines, Beatrice had turned to look at Blood Mountain. She could just make out what looked like narrow railroad tracks winding up its side and ending at the mouth of a tunnel. Then Beatrice saw something that made her blood turn cold. An enormous figure was standing at the entrance to the tunnel. It was at least twenty feet tall and its skin was a hideous green-gray color that reminded Beatrice of mold. Its head was large and misshapen, and its massive arms hung down to its knees. The creature was wearing a short ragged shift and it gripped a menacing-looking club in one fist.

"That must be one of the Ghumbabas," Beatrice said, staring in horror at the awful thing.

"Grotesque, isn't it?" Ollie said.

Cayenne leaped to Beatrice's shoulder and crouched down, peering up at the tunnel guard through slitted eyes. Beatrice could feel Cayenne's heart beating fast, and she reached up to stroke the cat.

Teddy and Cyrus had their eyes glued to the giant, as well.

"And we have to face *that?*" Cyrus muttered under his breath.

But Beatrice's attention had wandered elsewhere. At the base of the mountain was a line of carts that she assumed were used to carry the gnomes up the tracks to the tunnel. *If we could reach the mine entrance*, Beatrice thought, *maybe there's a way to the top* inside *the mountain.* She glanced back at the giant, and then at the relatively small mouth of the tunnel. There was no way the Ghumbabas could follow them into the mines.

About that time, Beatrice heard shouting and turned her attention back to Winged-Horse Mountain. The fire was still blazing. Seamus and a young man with dark shoulder-length hair were starting up the cliff. Both men were shouting instructions to the gnomes.

But the gnomes had stopped moving and were staring hopelessly at the rapidly spreading fire. The young man was still climbing toward them, but suddenly he tripped— and went sliding down the mountainside into Seamus's legs.

Joy cried out when the man fell. But now she saw him struggling to his feet, and said, "Thank goodness, he's all right." She glanced at Beatrice, and then looked back at the mountain. "That's my brother, Paxton. He's the mine foreman, so the gnomes report to him."

They watched as Paxton started back up the mountain.

"He's going to get hurt," Joy said, her face tight with worry. "Why don't they just give up and come down?"

Beatrice had noticed bits of fiery brush blowing off the mountain toward the ranch. It occurred to her that the fire might end up spreading to the buildings.

"I can take care of it," Beatrice said hastily.

Joy gave Beatrice a surprised look. "Then do it," she said.

Beatrice began to chant:

> *Circle of magic, hear my plea,*
> *Gentle rain,*
> *Falling free,*
> *This, I ask you, bring to me.*

Instantly, a steady rain began to fall on Winged-Horse Mountain and on the heads of the onlookers.

Joy stared at Beatrice in amazement. Then she turned back to the mountain and exclaimed, "Look! The fire's going out."

Beatrice was relieved to see that the flames did, indeed, seem to be growing smaller. With rain pelting her face, she watched as Seamus, Paxton, and all the gnomes trooped happily down the mountain. A young man with blond hair, wearing jeans and holding a white Stetson, waited for them at the bottom.

"Who's the good-looking guy with the cowboy hat?" Teddy asked.

"That's Uri Luna," Joy answered. "He's director of the summer camp, and he gives riding lessons to our guests."

Teddy was grinning. "I could use a few riding lessons," she said brightly.

Beatrice rolled her eyes and then looked back at the mountain, just as Paxton and Seamus reached Uri Luna. The fair-haired riding instructor reached out to help Seamus over a pile of stones, but Beatrice noticed that he turned sharply away from Paxton, literally giving Joy's brother the cold shoulder.

I wonder what he has against Paxton, Beatrice thought. Then she noticed another figure standing under the trees near the gnome village. It was Orion. Joy caught sight of the hunter and waved to him. Orion raised his bow slightly in response before turning away and disappearing into the copse of trees.

Seamus was directing the gnomes to clean up the charred brush that had fallen from the mountain and Uri was piling up the blackened skeletons of bushes that were too large for the diminutive miners. Paxton watched Uri intently for a moment, frowning, and then walked away. He came over to where his sister was standing.

"It's nearly out," Paxton said, the gray eyes that were so much like Joy's scanning the mountain. "If this rain keeps up a little while longer, we'll be okay."

"I'm sure Beatrice can arrange that," Joy said with a smile in Beatrice's direction.

Paxton gave his sister a quizzical look. "What are you talking about?"

"Beatrice, I'd like to introduce my brother, Paxton Rowntree," Joy said. "Pax, this is our new guest, Beatrice Bailey. She cast a spell for rain—and just in time, I'd say."

Paxton shook Beatrice's hand and nodded gravely. "We were having a hard time putting it out. I was afraid it was going to spread to the ranch."

Beatrice introduced her companions—including Ira, who was complaining loudly about being drenched—and then she said to Paxton, "Joy told us that you're the mine foreman."

"That's right." Paxton's jaw tightened and he added bitterly, "I'm one of Dally Rumpe's slaves."

"Paxton," Joy said quickly, "you're no such thing."

Paxton scowled. "He owns me as surely as he owns the gnomes."

Joy sighed. Then to Beatrice she said, "The last foreman treated the miners badly. When he left, Paxton agreed to take the job because he wanted to help the gnomes. And he has!"

"There's little enough I can do," Paxton muttered, his eyes moving restlessly to where Uri was still helping to clear away debris. "They lead miserable lives."

Ignoring his dark mood, Beatrice said, "You must know the mine tunnels pretty well."

"I'm not allowed on the mountain," he replied curtly. "Only gnomes with special papers can get past the Ghumbabas."

"If it's such a hard life," Ollie said suddenly, "why do the gnomes work for Dally Rumpe?"

"Because they don't have a choice!" Angry color flooded Paxton's face. "Gnomes will never leave the place they were born, and there's no other work here except for the few jobs Joy can give them. It's either the mines or starve to death."

"These gnomes and their ancestors used to work for Bromwich," Joy explained. "They had good lives then because Bromwich was generous to them. They even got a share of the profits. But now they work long hours for very little pay."

Paxton was staring at Beatrice, his gray eyes hostile. "You're probably asking yourself why I would choose to work for Dally Rumpe. Unlike the gnomes, I'm free to leave Winged-Horse Mountain anytime I choose."

"You stay because I won't leave," Joy said hastily, "and you won't go without me."

Beatrice heard that deep sadness in her voice again. *What could have happened to cause such grief?* Beatrice wondered.

"And you work for Dally Rumpe to make the gnomes' lives easier," Joy finished softly.

Paxton looked as though he were about to explode. "Right," he snapped, his eyes blazing. "I'm a regular saint."

He turned abruptly and stalked through the rain toward the ranch house. Looking at Joy, Beatrice couldn't tell if it was raindrops or tears running down the older witch's face.

"He's so unhappy here," Joy said, watching her brother's retreating back. "Everyone at the ranch despises him because they think he's in cahoots with Dally Rumpe. But it's not that way at all," she added fiercely. "The only work he does for Dally Rumpe is supervising the miners."

By this time, Seamus and Uri Luna had joined them. Uri's face seemed to close up when he heard what Joy was saying.

Joy's eyes locked with Uri's. "I know you don't believe this," she said, her voice trembling with emotion, "but Paxton would never deliberately hurt anyone. He's a good man."

Uri's eyebrows lifted, as if he questioned the truth of this. Joy burst into tears and took off for the ranch house.

No one knew what to say—no one, that is, except Ira Skelly.

"She's a sensitive and caring person," Ira said, his pointed chin raised as he glared at Uri. "I'm going to make sure she's all right."

They all watched as he stomped across the yard after Joy.

Beatrice was flabbergasted by this turn of events. Of course, Joy was very nice, and exceptionally pretty, but who would have guessed that *any* woman could have turned stuffy Ira Skelly into a knight in shining armor?

"Things are looking up," Ollie said quietly to Beatrice.

"What do you mean?"

Ollie grinned. "Just that your tutor seems to have other things on his mind," he replied, "besides driving you crazy."

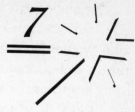

Omens

Now that the fire was out, the crowd was disassembling. Seamus went back inside without so much as a word of thanks to Beatrice, but Uri was still standing there, looking vaguely uncomfortable after Joy's outburst.

Beatrice brushed aside her wet bangs and mumbled a spell to stop the rain.

"That was really impressive," Uri said, staring at the clouds of steam that blanketed Winged-Horse Mountain. "We appreciate your help."

"It's no big deal," Beatrice replied.

"By the way, I'm Uri Luna," he said awkwardly. "If you and your friends would like some riding lessons while you're here, I'm your man."

A smiling Teddy sidled over. "Funny you should mention that," she said. "I was just saying that I'd *love* to learn to ride from an expert."

Uri seemed to think this was pretty amusing. Chuckling, he said, "We're planning a midnight ride and cookout in the desert later this week. I hope you'll all come."

"We'll be there," Teddy answered emphatically.

"Sounds like fun," Beatrice said, but her mind was on other things. She was thinking that Uri seemed nice enough, but he obviously didn't like Paxton Rowntree. Was it only because Paxton had taken a job from Dally Rumpe, or was there more to it than that?

Just then, Kasper Cloud came running up and grabbed hold of Uri's arm. "You promised to give me a private riding lesson," he said.

"Don't you have arts and crafts now?" Uri asked him.

Ignoring the question, Kasper said, "It probably wouldn't help, anyway. I don't think I'll ever learn to ride."

"You've improved already," Uri assured him, bringing a hesitant smile to the young witch's solemn face. "You just have to keep at it."

Beatrice noticed that Kasper seemed to like Uri, and the riding instructor certainly had a way with kids.

"I'll meet you at the stables at four," Uri promised Kasper. "But right now you're supposed to be making a leather belt."

"I'm all thumbs at that, too," Kasper said, and took off for the ranch house.

"He doesn't have much confidence in himself, does he?" Beatrice said.

"Poor kid," Uri said softly. "His mother and father don't spend any time with him. They didn't even bring him to camp."

"Have you been at Winged-Horse Ranch long?" Ollie asked.

"All my life," Uri replied. "My father used to work for Seamus's father, so this has been home as long as I can remember."

"Then you must know a lot about Blood Mountain," Beatrice said.

Uri's face darkened. "I know that anyone who sets foot on that mountain is begging for trouble," he said bluntly. "Of course, I don't expect anything I say to discourage you. You have your heads set on climbing it, don't you?"

Beatrice and her friends nodded.

Uri's expression showed clearly that he thought they were nuts, but then he said, "If you insist on going, you'll need climbing equipment. Come on, we have some stuff in the stables you can borrow."

They followed him to the stables and into a storeroom. Uri opened a cabinet and began pulling out helmets, ropes, and picks.

Ollie looked doubtfully at all the paraphernalia and said, "I think we're going to need lessons in rock climbing, too."

Uri frowned. "I guess I could show you the basics on Winged-Horse Mountain," he said. "But I'm hoping you'll change your minds before then."

Beatrice was thanking Uri for his help when she noticed Cayenne saunter over to a bale of hay where a large black cat was sitting.

"That's Ambrose," Uri said, reaching out to scratch behind the big cat's ear. "He's in charge of mouse control around here."

Cayenne and Ambrose touched noses and sniffed. Then the black cat leaped to a ladder and scrambled up into the loft. Cayenne was starting after him when Beatrice grabbed her.

"You can come back later," Beatrice informed the displeased cat, "but right now I need a shower and a nap."

"I haven't seen any sign of Miranda," Beatrice said as she and her friends started downstairs for dinner. Ira was bounding ahead. *Breaking his neck to see Joy*, Beatrice thought in amusement.

"Me, either," Ollie replied. "Maybe they've found her by now."

"I certainly hope so," Teddy said emphatically. "This part of the test is going to be hard enough without worrying about *her*."

Dickens greeted them when they reached the dining room and led them to a table for six. Most of the other tables were already filled. Beatrice caught sight of Uri Luna, who was sitting with Kasper and several other campers, and there were Joy and Seamus sharing a table with a middle-aged woman who had dyed red hair and was wearing too much makeup. Ira sat down beside Beatrice, craning his neck for a better view of Joy.

A young woman with curly, blond hair brought them menus. "Merry meet," she said cheerfully. "My name is Fairlamb and I'll be your server tonight. Why don't you take a few minutes to look at your menus, and I'll be back to take your orders."

Cyrus opened the large menu with obvious trepidation. For him, the hardest part of their trips to the Sphere was having to deal with witch food.

"Salamander stew," Cyrus muttered. "Horned toad chilli and beans." He looked up and said mournfully, "No burgers, no hot dogs, no fries. I'm going to starve to death!"

"The grilled bat steak sounds good," Beatrice told him. "It probably tastes like beef."

"The giant's breath soup is a house specialty," Teddy said. "I'm going to have that and . . . the daylily salad with spider's web dressing."

"I'll try the katydid kebabs," Ollie said. "I wonder if the rattail soup is any good."

Cyrus's face had turned a pale green, but when Fairlamb returned to the table, he gritted his teeth and ordered the bat steak and a snapdragon salad.

While they ate, Beatrice became aware that the woman sitting with Joy and Seamus was staring at her.

"Who is that woman—the one with red hair?" Beatrice asked when Fairlamb came back to refill their glasses with horsefly tea.

"Oh, that's Hyacinth Broomshead," Fairlamb replied with a noticeable lack of enthusiasm. "She comes here several times a year. I think she's after Seamus," Fairlamb added in a lowered voice, before hurrying away to another table.

"That Broomshead woman is sure interested in you," Teddy said to Beatrice. "She hasn't taken her eyes off you since we sat down."

"She's probably read the newspaper articles and recognizes you," Ollie said.

"Don't look now," Teddy said, "but she's coming over here."

"So she is," Ira said, and leaped up from his chair. "I really should tell Seamus how much I'm enjoying myself."

Beatrice grinned as she watched the tutor stride over to Joy and Seamus's table, and then sit down in the chair that Hyacinth Broomshead had vacated.

Teddy giggled. "He's *so* transparent."

By now, Hyacinth had reached their table. The woman was wearing expensive silk robes in a garish shade of orange that clashed with her red hair. Rings with over-size stones flashed on every one of her plump fingers, and glittery earrings dangled to her shoulders. When she leaned closer, Beatrice noticed that her face seemed to be sagging under the weight of all that powder and rouge. This witch was a mess!

The woman was hovering over Beatrice with a scarlet smile that showed an alarming number of teeth.

"When I saw you, I just had to come over and intro-duce myself," she boomed at Beatrice. "I'm Hyacinth Broomshead—of the Talon's Point Broomsheads," she added, appearing certain that this would impress Beatrice.

The next thing Beatrice knew, the woman was pulling out the chair beside her, not seeming to notice that Cayenne was already sitting there. Beatrice scooped up a startled Cayenne just in time to save the cat from being crushed by Hyacinth's ample hips.

Hyacinth Broomshead scooted her chair up to the table, still directing that toothy smile at Beatrice. "I'm a great fan of yours," she announced, her voice carrying across the room. "What you've done is absolutely astounding. I told Seamus that I just *had* to come over and get your autograph."

With that, the witch thrust a pen and piece of paper at Beatrice. "Just write, 'To my dear friend Hyacinth,'" the woman dictated, " 'with warmest wishes—'"

Beatrice suppressed a sigh and began to write, aware that Teddy, Ollie, and Cyrus were trying hard not to laugh.

"'—and undying gratitude,'" Hyacinth continued, her face so close that Beatrice could feel the woman's hot breath on her neck. "'I couldn't have broken Dally Rumpe's spell without you.'"

Beatrice cut her eyes at the woman, but Hyacinth just beamed at her. "My friends back at Talon's Point will be *so* impressed," she gushed.

Beatrice and her companions were forced to endure another five minutes of Hyacinth's obnoxious chatter before she rose to return to her own table. They all watched as she crossed the room and came to stand behind Ira, expecting him to remove himself from her chair. But the tutor was listening with rapt attention to something Joy was saying and didn't budge. Finally, Seamus had to bring a chair from another table for Hyacinth.

"The pitfalls of fame," Ollie said, grinning at Beatrice.

"*Puh—lease,*" Beatrice muttered, rolling her eyes.

Cayenne had settled back in her chair and was scarfing down a large helping of salamander stew. The rest of them returned to their meals, as well, but it wasn't two minutes later when another guest appeared at their table.

Beatrice looked up to see a very old woman standing there. Dressed in neat gray robes, her silver hair pulled back into a knot at the nape of her neck, the woman was smiling sweetly at Beatrice.

This time, Ollie pulled up a chair for their visitor.

"Why, thank you, young man," the woman said softly, and sat down between him and Cayenne. "I hope I'm not disturbing you," she said with a sparkle in her blue eyes. "Your table seems to be getting a lot of attention."

"You aren't disturbing us," Beatrice assured her.

"I'm Winifred Stoop," the older witch said, reaching out to stroke Cayenne's head. "And I know who you are. Beatrice, Teddy, Cyrus, and Ollie," she said, her eyes lighting on each as she spoke their names. "And I know why you've come to Winged-Horse Mountain."

Beatrice smiled. "*Everyone* seems to," she said lightly.

"Have you been to Winged-Horse Ranch before?" Ollie asked the woman.

"Oh, my, yes," she replied. "I come back every year. You see, my deceased husband was a rodeo cowboy. After he died—more than forty years ago now—he joined the Phantom Rodeo."

Cyrus blinked. "You mean—like ghosts?"

Winifred laughed softly. "Exactly. Phantom cowboys riding phantom horses and roping phantom calves. The rodeo performs at Winged-Horse Mountain every summer, so I come back to see my Hector. They'll be here in a few days," she added. "You should go see them. It's quite a show!"

They all agreed that they wouldn't miss it.

"But you're probably wondering why I've interrupted your meal," Winifred said. "I have—a message, I suppose you would call it. Sometimes, in my dreams, I can see the future." She turned her gentle gaze on Beatrice. "And last night, I saw yours, my dear. I had to warn you."

Beatrice felt suddenly cold. "Warn me about what?" she asked.

"In my dream," Winifred said, watching Beatrice closely, "I saw you and your friends arriving on horseback at the ranch. And I saw omens that signify that you will face great difficulty. First, there was thunder. Then a black cat."

Teddy's eyes darted to Beatrice's face. "Balto created thunder and we saw that black cat in the stables."

"You may be thinking that this is just coincidence," Winifred said to Beatrice, "but my dreams never lie. Before the day ends, you will discover that three people are plotting against you, and you'll see a falling star—both ominous signs that must be taken seriously."

"Who are these three people?" Beatrice asked quickly.

Winifred shook her head. "They were surrounded by dense fog, and I couldn't see who they were. But I received a very strong message that I need to relay to you. I saw you being faced with the most important decision of your life, thus far. You will have to choose between good and evil. Of course," the woman went on, "you believe that you would always choose good, but you can't be certain of that this time. Evil may not be as clearly defined as you imagine."

Beatrice wasn't sure what to make of this. Winifred seemed both kind and sincere—but also a little odd. Maybe she *had* dreamed about Beatrice, but who knew whether she was actually seeing into the future?

Noting Beatrice's frown, Winifred smiled her understanding. "You're thinking that I might be just a silly old woman making too much of her dreams. And why shouldn't you? You don't know me, after all. But it's very important, Beatrice, that you take this dream seriously. Be prepared to face the decision I mentioned—and try hard to make the right choice."

Beatrice nodded, not wanting to hurt the woman's feelings with her doubts. "Thank you for telling me," she said politely.

"And one other thing," Winifred added. "See that man at the table in the corner?"

Beatrice's eyes followed Winifred's. She saw a distinguished-looking man dressed in rich royal-blue robes. His white hair and beard were luminous in the candlelight. And he was staring at Beatrice.

"His name is Marco Bell," Winifred said. "He's been a guest here for a couple of days, and I dreamed about him, as well. The dream was jumbled, but I can tell you this, Beatrice: You shouldn't trust him. Because Marco Bell isn't what he appears to be."

Beatrice followed her friends up the stairs and stifled a yawn as she said good night to Ollie and Cyrus. It had been a long, tiring day, and she was ready for bed. But as she headed for the bathroom with her gown and slippers, she noticed that her watch was missing. She came back into the bedroom, where Teddy was taking clothes from her backpack and placing them in a drawer.

"Have you seen my watch?" Beatrice asked, her eyes on the floor as she retraced her steps to the hall.

"The one your parents gave you for your birthday?" Teddy asked. "Don't tell me you've lost it."

"Looks that way," Beatrice said, trying not to sound as upset as she felt. That watch meant a lot to her, and she couldn't remember the last time she had seen it on her wrist. What if it had fallen off when they were flying over the desert? In that case, she'd *never* find it.

Then Beatrice realized that her cat was missing, as well.

"Wasn't Cayenne with us when we came upstairs?" Beatrice asked sharply.

She dropped to her knees and peered under the bed. When she sat up again, her face registered worry and confusion. "What's going on?" she mumbled. Could someone have taken her watch *and* her cat?

Teddy looked under her own bed. "She isn't here."

Suddenly Beatrice leaped to her feet. "Ambrose!" she exclaimed, and started for the door. "I'll bet Cayenne's gone to the stables."

"Wait," Teddy said, rushing after her. "I'll go with you."

They left by the back door and started toward the stables. Winged-Horse Mountain had disappeared under the cover of darkness, but the peaks of Blood Mountain stood out like burning embers against the blackened sky, its red sun seeming to sizzle overhead.

"*That* is definitely eery," Teddy muttered, and looked away from the crimson glow.

When they entered the stables, Beatrice heard a man's voice. She couldn't tell who it was, or hear what he was saying, because he was speaking softly; but she sensed the urgency behind his words.

Beatrice put a finger to her lips and began to move silently toward the storeroom door, which stood open a few inches, allowing a sliver of light to spill out into the dark corridor.

As they approached the door, they heard a woman's voice. Beatrice realized at once that it was Fairlamb, and she sounded upset.

Beatrice eased up to the door, with Teddy close behind her. They peered through the crack, holding their breaths. Yes, there stood Fairlamb, and with her were two men—Uri Luna and Marco Bell.

This is really strange, Beatrice thought. Hadn't Winifred Stoop said that Marco Bell was a new guest? So what was he doing in the stables, at night, with two ranch employees?

Now Uri was speaking, his voice carrying clearly to Beatrice and Teddy's ears.

"Of course we trust you, Fairlamb," Uri said, sounding impatient, "but you shouldn't be involved in this. You wouldn't be if you hadn't been such a snoop."

"I'm *not* a snoop," Fairlamb responded with obvious indignation. "And you *can* trust me. I'm not about to tell Beatrice Bailey *anything*."

Beatrice felt her knees go weak. Winifred had said that before the day was over Beatrice would discover three people plotting against her. And here they were: Uri, Fairlamb, and Marco Bell.

"We'd better call it a night," Uri was saying, "before someone sees us."

Teddy clutched Beatrice's arm tightly, and the two of them moved away as quickly and quietly as possible. Beatrice noticed a large wooden feed bin and ducked behind it. Teddy dove in after her.

The light in the storeroom went out, the door clicked shut, and the three conspirators filed by, unaware that Beatrice and Teddy were hiding only inches away.

When the outside door shut, Beatrice sank to the floor, questions swirling inside her head.

"This was right out of Winifred's prophecy," Teddy said softly. "Now all we need is a shooting star."

"But who are these people?" Beatrice demanded. "And why are they plotting against me?"

"I don't know," Teddy admitted, "but we're going to find out."

Just then, Beatrice felt something brush against her leg. A startled cry rose in her throat, but then she felt a cat's silky fur beneath her outstretched hand.

"Cayenne?" Beatrice said hoarsely, and was answered with a familiar meow.

"Don't you know how worried I was?" Beatrice chided the cat. "The next time you decide to visit Ambrose, let me know, okay?"

"But if she hadn't come out to the stables," Teddy said reasonably, "we wouldn't have known about those three meeting here."

And exactly what do we know? Beatrice wondered as she and Teddy left the stables, with Cayenne snuggled serenely in her arms.

They were crossing the yard toward the ranch house when Beatrice happened to look up. She saw a ribbon of silver against the deep velvet sky, the path of a star as it fell to earth.

8

The Lost Witch

Teddy and Cayenne had been asleep for over an hour, but Beatrice was still tossing and turning, her mind whirling with thoughts of black cats and falling stars, and the disturbing meeting she had witnessed in the stables. *Are Uri, Fairlamb, and Marco Bell working for Dally Rumpe?* she wondered. *Could one of them be Dally Rumpe?*

Beatrice finally gave up on sleep and sat down at the writing table to read the history chapters Ira had assigned. Through the window, she could see the crimson peaks of Blood Mountain rising up out of the darkness, and they appeared more ominous than ever. Then she saw something flying above the mountain. It was Balto, his white coat tinged pink by the fierce red sun.

After reading a few pages, Beatrice realized she was hungry. She had skipped dessert, but now she was remembering how good the lemon thyme custard had looked. She didn't think anyone would mind if she went down to the kitchen for a snack.

Beatrice opened the door to the hall cautiously so as not to wake Teddy and Cayenne, and then made her way down the hall to the stairs, her dragon slippers slapping against the tile floor. Once she reached the kitchen, there was no need to turn on the overhead light because the room was suffused with a dull red glow from the sun over Blood Mountain.

Beatrice opened the huge refrigerator and saw a tray of dessert dishes filled with custard. She helped herself to one, found a spoon, and sat down at the table to enjoy her snack. She was eating blissfully when she heard a thump outside the kitchen door.

Beatrice froze, spoon poised, as she listened to the faint sound of footsteps crossing the back porch. She lowered her spoon to the table and stood up. Through the panes of glass in the door, she could see a figure descending the steps. Beatrice crept silently to the door and peered out, her heart thrashing wildly in her chest. The figure had disappeared into the darkness, but a small bundle had been left in one of the porch chairs.

Suddenly the room was filled with blinding light. Beatrice spun around—and found herself staring into Joy's startled face. The older witch was clutching the front of her robe, one hand still on the light switch.

"*Beatrice!*" Joy exclaimed, and let out a shaky breath. "You scared me to death."

"Ditto," Beatrice answered weakly.

Joy's eyes moved to the dessert dish and she looked relieved. "I thought I heard a noise outside."

"Someone *was* there," Beatrice said, "and whoever it was left something on the porch."

Joy was already heading for the door. She stepped outside and returned with a bulging burlap sack.

"It was just Orion," Joy said, "a hunter who lives up on Winged-Horse Mountain. He brings us fresh game and, in exchange, I leave him some of whatever I've cooked that day. He seems especially fond of my horned-toad chilli."

Beatrice watched as Joy made room in the freezer for the meat.

"This Orion seems pretty mysterious," Beatrice said thoughtfully. "Who is he, anyway?"

Joy shrugged. "I don't really know. He just showed up one day. I usually only see him at night, and he always has that hood pulled down over his face, so I can't even tell you what he looks like."

Beatrice was suspicious of the hunter, a feeling she didn't like very much. Before the Executive Committee had presented her with this test, she had been a trusting person; but now she seemed to be always questioning someone's motives, and suspecting anyone she didn't know of ill intent. Even so, Orion was a mystery, and, therefore, not above suspicion. For all Beatrice knew, he might even be Dally Rumpe.

"I think he's quite old, and he must have had a sad past," Joy was saying, and Beatrice could hear the woman's own sorrow in her voice. "No one would live as he does, alone in a cave, if they hadn't been badly treated by life. But there's goodness in him," Joy added quietly. "I can feel it."

Beatrice woke up, slumped over the writing table, with the sun streaming in through the window. She sat up, her stiff back resisting anything more than a gentle stretch. Glancing at the clock, she saw that it was 5:45. Teddy and Cayenne were still asleep.

Beatrice felt groggy, but she knew that she would never be able to go back to sleep. She pulled a pair of shorts and a T-shirt from her backpack and went to take a shower.

A few minutes later, Beatrice left Teddy and Cayenne still sleeping and went down to the dining room. A sign indicated that breakfast wouldn't be served until 6:30, so Beatrice sat down in the lobby to wait.

Through the front window, she could see a lot of activity around Blood Mountain. Gnomes were piling into the carts at its base, while others were already being transported up the tracks to the mine's entrance. Paxton was there, too, apparently shouting out orders to the gnomes who were still on the ground.

"You're up early," came a voice from behind Beatrice.

She looked around to find Uri Luna standing there. Now that she knew he was keeping secrets from her, Beatrice didn't feel especially friendly toward the riding instructor. But since she didn't want him to know that she had seen him meeting with Fairlamb and Marco Bell, Beatrice smiled and tried to sound natural when she said good morning.

If her greeting was a little too exuberant, Uri didn't seem to notice. He was looking past her, appearing interested in something he saw through the window.

"I guess you've been told that we have ruby mines here," Uri said, his gaze still directed outside. "Or I should say, *Dally Rumpe* has ruby mines. No one else sees a penny of profit from them. Well—*most* of us don't, anyway," he added stiffly.

Beatrice followed his gaze and saw Paxton talking to the last group of gnomes before they started up the mountain. "Do you think Paxton gets a share of the profits?" Beatrice asked casually.

Uri jerked his head toward her, obviously caught off guard. But he recovered quickly and replied pleasantly enough, "I have no idea. But there must be *some* reason why he'd work for Dally Rumpe."

"Maybe he just wants to help the gnomes," Beatrice suggested.

Uri's jaw tightened. "You've been listening to Joy," he said, sounding faintly accusing. "Of course, she has to believe that her brother wouldn't do anything wrong."

"But you think otherwise?"

"I'm not paid to analyze the other witches at Winged-Horse Ranch," he said, curt to the point of rudeness. "Let me know if you want those riding lessons," he added, and headed for the door.

Beatrice was still thinking about Uri's obvious hostility toward Paxton when her friends and Ira came downstairs for breakfast. As she dug into a tall stack of zucchini pancakes with honeyed-ant syrup, Beatrice watched Fairlamb move efficiently from table to table.

"She *seems* nice enough," Beatrice muttered.

"Who seems nice?" Cyrus asked, looking up from his bowl of hot cereal. The breakfast menu had been too much for him, and he'd settled for oatmeal with dragon's milk.

"Fairlamb," Teddy answered before Beatrice could, and began to tell Cyrus and Ollie about seeing the waitress in the stables with Uri and Marco Bell.

Ira didn't seem to be paying attention to the conversation. He was too busy casting wistful glances at Joy, who was sitting across the room with Winifred Stoop. Even so, Beatrice wasn't comfortable with Teddy speaking so openly in front of him. After all, Ira was a stranger. How did they know what he might be up to?

Near the end of the meal, Joy stood up and asked for everyone's attention.

"We have two special events planned this morning," she announced. "For those of you who'd like a closer look at Blood Mountain, Seamus will be leading a walking tour around its base. And I'll be taking anyone interested in doing a little shopping into the nearby town of Tombstone. We'll meet you in the lobby in fifteen minutes."

"I think I'll go into town," Ira said promptly. "I need—dental floss."

Teddy snickered, and then mouthed the words *dental floss?* to Beatrice.

Ira turned to Beatrice, as if suddenly remembering her existence, and said brusquely, "Have you finished your assignment?"

"You said I had until dinnertime," Beatrice reminded him.

"So you're going to wait till the last minute?" Ira asked sternly. "You'd better stay in today and concentrate on studying."

"When werewolves fly," Beatrice muttered.

But Ira didn't hear her. He was already making a beeline for Joy's table.

Beatrice sighed. She had three chapters left to read—and the first chapter to reread, since she couldn't remember anything about it at the moment. Okay, so she was a little behind on the assignment. But why did Ira have to be so *mean?*

"I think we should go on the walking tour," she said as they left the dining room. "Maybe we'll learn something useful about Blood Mountain."

"But don't you need to study?" Ollie asked.

Beatrice scowled at him. "Has Ira made you his second in command?" she asked curtly.

Ollie just shrugged, but Beatrice could see that his feelings were hurt, and immediately regretted being short with him. But before she could apologize, Hyacinth Broomshead came swooping down on her.

"Beatrice, are you going into town with Joy?" the older witch asked in her booming voice. "We'll finally have some time to talk."

"My friends and I are going on the walking tour," Beatrice answered quickly.

Hyacinth's heavily rouged face fell. "That's too bad," she said. "But I suppose we can get together later."

"Sure," Beatrice said, easing away from the woman. "Well . . . have a good time in Tombstone."

"I know I will," Hyacinth said jauntily. "I'm going to buy some authentic Western jewelry."

"Not rings, I hope," Ollie said under his breath as Hyacinth waved a bejeweled hand and hurried out the door.

"Wow," Cyrus said softly.

About thirty people had gone on the walking tour, including Uri and many of the campers, and now they stood at the foot of Blood Mountain staring up at the massive sculpture of Dally Rumpe's head.

"It took more than twenty years to carve this," Seamus was saying in the practiced manner of a professional tour guide. "Dally Rumpe had sculptors brought in from all over the Sphere to do the work. They say this is a perfect likeness."

Beatrice squinted against the red glare of the stone at the finely chiseled features of the sorcerer. In the sculpture, he appeared young and handsome, as he had in a portrait she had seen at Sea-Dragon Bay. But Beatrice had been face-to-face with Dally Rumpe, and knew that he was anything but handsome. The image that came unbidden in her dreams was monstrous!

"Oooh—*Look!*" exclaimed one of the campers. "Under Dally Rumpe's face!"

Beatrice's eyes shifted from the sorcerer's stone image to a giant that was lumbering along a rocky ledge in the shadow of Dally Rumpe's chin. Up close, the creature appeared even more grotesque—not to mention more intimidating. Beatrice looked at his enormous hand and knew that those doughy gray fingers could squeeze the life out of a witch in an instant.

Seamus brought their attention back to the sculpture by describing all the different tools and spells used to create it. When he finally paused for breath, Kasper walked up to him.

"But why did Dally Rumpe want his face on a mountain out here in the middle of nowhere?" the boy asked.

"I've heard this mountain has personal significance for Dally Rumpe," Seamus replied.

"What kind of significance?"

"No one knows that," Seamus said impatiently.

"*Someone* must," Kasper persisted.

Seamus was scowling down at the boy. "*Someone* may, but *I* don't," he snapped.

Uri had walked up, and now he placed an arm around Kasper's shoulders. "Look at that rattler, buddy," he said, gently drawing the boy away from Seamus and pointing toward the mountain.

Beatrice spotted the large brown snake sunning itself on a pile of rocks and shuddered. But Kasper was still looking pensively at Seamus.

"He's almost as grouchy as my dad," Kasper remarked. "My mom says Dad's just tired because he works too hard, but that's not it. He gets mad at me because I'm not good at anything."

"Maybe he has a lot on his mind," Uri suggested.

But the young witch was thinking hard and didn't seem to hear him.

"One time," Kasper said, frowning as he remembered, "Dad said to me, 'I had high expectations for you, boy, but you've let me down more times than I can count. I'm gravely disappointed in you.'"

Overhearing this conversation, Beatrice felt sorry for Kasper—and angry at his father. What kind of parent would say something like that to his child?

"Sometimes people say hurtful things because they're unhappy themselves," Uri was saying, "but they aren't bad people. Take Seamus," he added, looking over the heads of other campers at the ranch owner. "I've known him all my life, and I can tell you, Kasper, he's a gentle, caring witch at heart."

"Then why is he so crabby?" Kasper asked.

Uri hesitated, then said quietly, "Seamus's son, Dominy, died last year. Dominy and I grew up together, and we were good friends. But he wasn't like most of the other boys around here. He was quiet—you know, more serious than the rest of us—and he wasn't interested in riding or hiking. He'd rather read a book."

"Like me," Kasper said quickly.

"Some of the boys thought Dominy was a sissy," Uri continued, his eyes clouded as he remembered. "They used to tease him all the time. Dominy never said anything, but I could tell it gnawed at him. I used to say, 'Who cares what they think? They're just being stupid, you know?' But it still bothered him."

"So what did he do?" Kasper asked eagerly.

"He grew up," Uri said, "as we all did. And he fell in love with a pretty girl, and they decided to get married. But before the wedding, Dominy wanted to prove something—to himself and to those boys who had called him a coward. He decided to climb Blood Mountain to show how brave he really was."

Beatrice and her friends had moved closer and were all listening intently to Uri's story.

"Is that how he died?" Kasper asked softly.

Uri nodded, his face drawn. "Dominy went up on this mountain and never came back. All we ever found were pieces of his bloody robes strewn out over the desert." Uri sighed. "Anyway, since that time, Seamus has forgotten how to be kind. He's consumed with sorrow—and guilt, too, I expect. He thinks he should have been able to keep Dominy away from Blood Mountain."

Beatrice looked over at Seamus. Now that she knew about his son, she could see beyond the stern line of his mouth and the angry furrowing of his brow—to the grief that was eating away at him. *No wonder he's so against us climbing the mountain*, Beatrice thought.

"I couldn't help overhearing," she said to Uri. "I'm sorry about your friend."

Uri rubbed his face with both hands, as if he were very tired. Then he looked at her obliquely. "Thanks," he said. "But it was a lot harder for Dominy's father and fiancée than it was for me."

"Would we know his fiancée?" Beatrice asked.

"Sure," Uri replied. "It was Joy Rowntree."

So that's why she's so sad, Beatrice thought.

"And the boys who teased Dominy?"

"Most of them have moved away." Uri frowned, as if trying to decide whether to leave it at that or say more. "Joy's brother was one of them," he said finally. "After Dominy was killed, Paxton came to me and said that he was sorry, that he had never meant for it to end this way. But it was too late then," Uri added bitterly. "Dominy was gone. We'd already lost him to this mountain."

When they returned from the walking tour, Teddy, Ollie, and Cyrus decided to take a swim. Beatrice would have liked nothing better than to dive into that cool blue water, but she knew she couldn't put off studying any longer.

"I hate leaving you here all by yourself," Ollie said.

"It's okay," Beatrice replied, trying to sound as if she didn't mind. "I'll get a lot done before lunch."

After they were gone, Beatrice went into the bathroom to wash her hot face, and that's when she realized that her hair clip was missing. It was one of her favorites, an enameled cat that reminded her of Cayenne.

"I'm losing everything," Beatrice muttered as she came back into the bedroom. "First my watch, now my hair clip."

Cayenne was curled up on the bed, already asleep. Beatrice gave her an envious look, and then settled down at the writing table with her history book.

She tried to concentrate on what she was reading, but it was hard. She had a clear view of the pool from here, and she could see Teddy, Ollie, and Cyrus laughing and having a wonderful time.

Beatrice read a couple of paragraphs and then looked up again, just in time to see Cyrus push Teddy off the diving board and into the water. Beatrice grinned, knowing that Teddy would be out for blood. Then she heard a noise in the hall.

Beatrice looked toward the sound and was surprised to see the doorknob turning. It couldn't be Teddy—Beatrice had just seen her hit the water—and surely a maid would knock.

The door began to open slowly, and Beatrice felt a jolt of adrenaline rush through her body. Without pausing to think, she dropped to the floor and crouched down behind the bed.

The door creaked as it opened wider. Peering around the foot of the bed, Beatrice could see silky blue robes shimmering in the light from the window. As the intruder stepped into the room, Beatrice caught sight of a white beard. It was Marco Bell!

He closed the door behind him and Beatrice crouched lower. It never occurred to her to confront him because his reason for being here had to be sinister. People with honorable intentions didn't sneak into someone else's room!

Her face only inches from the floor, Beatrice couldn't see him now, but she could hear each step he took as he came slowly toward the bed.

Beatrice's heart was pounding. Any moment now he would see her cringing there. A desperate plan began to form in her mind. She could leap up at him, perhaps startling him enough so that she'd be able to bound across the bed and run for the door. But when she lifted her head, Beatrice realized that it was already too late for that.

Marco Bell was standing at the end of the bed. When he saw her, he made a sound like a surprised grunt deep in his throat.

Then everything happened at once. Beatrice screamed and leaped to her feet, Cayenne woke with a strangled yowl, and Teddy burst into the room shouting Beatrice's name.

Marco Bell spun around at the sound of Teddy's voice, and Beatrice threw her body against his. They both tumbled to the floor, with Beatrice on top. He was flailing his arms and kicking in an attempt to get away, but Beatrice struggled mightily to hold him down. All she could think was, *He's awfully strong for an old man!*

9

Witch in Disguise

Marco Bell made a jab at Beatrice's face, but Teddy grabbed hold of his clenched fist before it made contact with Beatrice's jaw. This seemed to infuriate the man. He let out a howl and started kicking with a vengeance. Beatrice was tossed and jolted by his twisting body, but she was determined to keep him pinned down. The two wrestled in a tangle of arms and legs across the floor, crashing into the writing table, turning over the chair. Beatrice's arms were beginning to tremble, and she was wondering how much longer she could hold on, when she felt Marco Bell's body suddenly go limp. Like Beatrice, he was breathing hard and didn't seem to have the strength to keep fighting.

"Find Seamus," Beatrice said to Teddy between pants. "Tell him—"

But before she could finish, Marco Bell swung an arm at her, catching her on the shoulder. Beatrice groaned and jerked back in pain, giving the man his chance to roll away from her.

But Beatrice wasn't about to let him escape now. She reached out for him with both hands, her fingers grasping his snowy beard.

What happened next was so totally unexpected, Beatrice gasped. The beard came off! She pulled her hands back in horror, and the fluffy white pelt fell to the floor.

Beatrice and Teddy screamed in unison. Then Beatrice's head jerked up so that she was face-to-face with the beardless Marco Bell. She was looking straight into a pair of pale gray eyes—and in a moment of shock, she realized that she had seen those eyes many times before.

"Miranda," Beatrice said.

"*What?*" A stunned Teddy dropped to her knees and stared into the intruder's face.

Miranda Pengilly, her lips curved into a smug half smile, stared right back at her.

About that time, the door from the hall opened, and Ollie and Cyrus came running in.

"We could hear screaming all the way from the stairs," Ollie said breathlessly. Then he took in the three girls sitting on the floor and blinked.

"Oh, my gosh," he muttered.

Cyrus was looking hard at Miranda. "Why, you're—" He swallowed, unable to speak the name.

Miranda sat back calmly and pulled the white wig off her head, revealing dark hair that was cut very short. She looked profoundly pleased with herself as she took in the astonished—and vaguely appalled—faces around her.

"So," Miranda said with a glint of triumph, "long time no see."

She was just as beautiful as Beatrice remembered—tall and slender, with perfect features, and those startling eyes that were so pale they looked almost silver. Miranda was regarding them steadily, her chin lifted slightly in that superior pose that Beatrice knew so well. Even after three months at The Rightpath School, she was the same old Miranda.

"What are you doing here?" Beatrice asked, having recovered a little from the initial shock. She was frowning as she rubbed her aching shoulder. "Don't you know that everyone in the Sphere is looking for you? And they probably know that you'll be wherever I am."

Miranda's eyebrows lifted mockingly. "As if I don't have better things to do than follow my famous little cousin around?"

"Well, you're here, aren't you?" Cyrus declared indignantly.

Beatrice's eyes narrowed suspiciously as she studied Miranda's face. "What is it you want?" she asked bluntly.

"I want to help you."

"Sure you do," Beatrice responded.

Miranda laughed. "I know, I wasn't all that helpful before. But I came through in the end, didn't I?"

"You saved my life," Beatrice admitted. "But if you're here to help, why didn't you let us know who you were right away? Why sneak into my room like you were coming to attack me?"

"I couldn't just walk up to you in the dining room and say, 'Hi there, Beatrice. Remember me?' You've been surrounded by people ever since you arrived, so I had to wait till we could talk privately. When I saw your partners in crime at the pool," she continued sarcastically, "I thought you might be up here alone for a change."

"You could have knocked," Beatrice said.

"I could have," Miranda agreed, and then smiled mischievously. "But that wouldn't have been any fun. I really enjoy the element of surprise."

Beatrice wasn't amused. Or convinced. But what choice did she have but to hear Miranda out? It wasn't like she was going to call the authorities and turn her cousin in. At least, not until she had a better idea of why Miranda was here.

"So you want to help us," Beatrice said. "Is that the only reason you left school?"

Miranda snorted. "Some school. It was a prison! Everything was ugly and gray, including the robes we had to wear. And anything I wanted to do was against the rules. So my leaving had nothing to do with you."

Beatrice thought Miranda was being truthful about this, anyway.

"You wouldn't believe the kids in that place," Miranda went on. "Some of them had done awful things."

"More awful than giving people witch fever?" Teddy asked coldly. "Or causing their balloon to crash into the sea? Or sending in an army of vicious rats—?"

"Okay, okay," Miranda cut in, "I *was* terrible. But I've changed. I realized while I was locked up in that place that I didn't want to be a bad witch anymore."

Teddy was staring at her with open distrust and animosity. Beatrice seemed to be thinking over what she had said.

"I really can help you," Miranda said to Beatrice. "I spent a lot of time with Dally Rumpe, so I know things about him that most people don't."

"Do you know if he's here at the ranch?" Beatrice asked.

Miranda shook her head. "I haven't recognized him, but he can take on any appearance he chooses, so he might be here. That's one of the reasons I have to go on pretending to be Marco Bell. Dally Rumpe has to be furious with me for betraying him. And, of course," she added grimly, "someone might turn me in if they knew who I really was. Reporters have made the public think I'm some kind of monster."

"Now who would believe that?" Teddy demanded.

Miranda flashed her a nasty look before turning back to Beatrice. "You have to promise not to give me away," Miranda said, "and let me help you."

"I want to trust you, but I don't know if I can," Beatrice answered honestly.

Miranda nearly succeeded in hiding her annoyance. "Just give me a chance," she said stiffly, "and I'll prove that I'm on your side."

"In the meantime," Ollie said thoughtfully to Beatrice, "we'll be able to keep a closer eye on her if she's working with us."

Miranda didn't appear too pleased with his reasoning, but she kept her mouth shut.

"All right," Beatrice said, already wondering if she would live to regret this. "We'll keep your identity a secret, Miranda, but I want your word that you won't betray us again."

"I promise," Miranda replied solemnly.

Teddy grimaced and rolled her eyes to the ceiling.

"Oh, I almost forgot." Beatrice walked over to her backpack and reached inside one of its pockets. "I have something that belongs to you."

She sat down beside Miranda and held out her hand.

Miranda looked surprised to see the silver pentagram in Beatrice's outstretched palm. Then she smiled and reached for the charm. "Where did you find this?" she asked.

"In the cellar of my house."

Miranda had the good grace to look embarrassed. "Oh, yeah. I was down there."

"Helping us?" Beatrice asked dryly.

"Spying on you," Miranda admitted, and then added hastily, "but only because I wanted to find out if you were coming back to the Sphere. You're so wishy-washy, Beatrice, no one ever knows if you're going to see it through or not."

Beatrice gave her cousin an indignant look.

"Anyway, thanks for returning the charm," Miranda said, and slipped it into the pocket of her robes.

"One more thing," Beatrice said as Miranda began to put on the wig and beard. "I saw you and Fairlamb and Uri Luna in the stables last night. And I heard Uri warning Fairlamb not to tell me anything. What was that all about?"

Miranda smiled, still enjoying her secrets. "We weren't plotting against you, if that's what you think," she said. "Uri and his parents used to come to Sea-Dragon Bay every summer, and I've known him since I was a baby, so I decided to trust him. But little Fairlamb has a crush on Uri," Miranda added. "She followed him one night when he came to meet me, and we had to. tell her who I really was. What you overheard was Uri reminding her that she couldn't tell anyone that I was here, even you. I wanted to tell you myself."

Her answer sounded plausible. *But who can ever tell about Miranda?* Beatrice thought. And if Uri and Miranda were old friends, that might be one more reason to distrust *him*. For all Beatrice knew, the three of them could all be working with Dally Rumpe.

As Beatrice was dressing for dinner, she realized that Ira would be there shortly to collect the history questions she was supposed to have answered. And she hadn't even finished reading the chapters!

"I think I'll go down to dinner early," Beatrice said to Teddy, thinking that maybe she could avoid a lecture from Ira. Surely he wouldn't make a scene in front of the other guests.

Teddy glanced at the history book on Beatrice's bed and grinned. "They won't be serving dinner for half an hour. Shouldn't you be studying?"

Beatrice frowned and blew her bangs out of her eyes. "I've been shut up in this room all afternoon," she grumbled, "not to mention being roughed up by—Marco Bell. I'm going to sit by the pool and relax."

The reference to Miranda was all it took to arouse Teddy's sympathy. "I'll go with you," she said, "and beat Ira off with a stick if he comes anywhere near us."

But Beatrice, Teddy, and Cayenne were only halfway down the stairs when Ira caught up with them.

"I'll take your assignment now," he said curtly, and held out his hand.

"You'll have it tonight," Beatrice replied, brushing past him and continuing down the stairs.

Ira hurried after her, his mouth set in a thin line. "That won't do," he snapped. "You knew the questions were to be turned in to me before dinner."

"I—got tied up this afternoon," Beatrice answered vaguely. They had reached the lobby and Beatrice was desperate to get away from him. She started toward the front door. "I'll finish the questions after dinner," she said over her shoulder.

Ira didn't like being dismissed, and it showed in his face. "You're wasting my time!" he shouted to her back. "I'd hate to have to contact Dr. Featherstone and tell her you aren't taking this seriously."

Beatrice's face flooded with color and she spun around to face him. "Do what you have to do," she said through clenched teeth, "but don't expect any support from Dr. Featherstone. She doesn't care if I pass American history or not!"

Their eyes were locked in open warfare. Ira was all set to express his fury when he saw Joy coming down the stairs. He clamped his mouth shut and turned away sharply from Beatrice.

"Merry meet," Ira said to Joy, and Beatrice watched in disgust as the anger in his face melted away, replaced by an unbelievably silly smile.

"Good grief," Teddy muttered.

"Sickening, isn't it?" Beatrice said under her breath. "But at least he's off my case."

"I was wondering if you would have dinner with me tonight," Ira was saying to Joy, practically drooling with eagerness. "I want to tell you about the work I'm doing. Maybe you can help me."

"Uh—I suppose so," Joy replied without much enthusiasm.

As Beatrice watched them head for the dining room, she heard a rumble of thunder. She and Teddy looked out the window and saw a flash of lightning. And there was Balto, his wings spread wide as he pawed the earth on top of Winged-Horse Mountain.

"Not again," Beatrice said, and then she saw the brush catch fire.

Joy ran outside, and the others followed. The gnomes were already gathering at the base of the mountain with their buckets.

Joy sighed and looked at Beatrice. "Would you mind?" she asked.

"Not at all," Beatrice replied, and started to chant.

A steady rain began to fall, and the gnomes turned to Beatrice, grinning and applauding. The flames hissed, growing smaller and smaller as they were doused with rain. Flying over the highest peak, Balto snorted with displeasure. He circled the mountain, and then, with an angry kick of his back legs, flew off toward Blood Mountain.

Blinking the rain from her eyes, Beatrice watched as Balto landed on top of the mountain. At the same moment, she saw something that made her gasp. One of the giants was hiding behind some boulders only a few yards away from the horse, where Balto couldn't see him! Suddenly the giant stood up, a dark silhouette against the blood-red stone, and began to twirl a rope over his head.

"Balto!" Beatrice screamed.

The horse's head turned toward her, but it was too late. The giant's rope had already landed around Balto's neck.

10

Miranda's Secret

The giant lumbered toward Balto, reeling in his prize, while the horse reared up on his hind legs and neighed angrily as the rope tightened around his neck.

Beatrice and Teddy stared at the scene in disbelief. From her perch on Beatrice's shoulder, Cayenne emitted a distressed yowl.

"I can't bear to watch this," Joy murmured, turning away with a pained expression. "They've tried and tried to catch him before, but he's always managed to get away."

A crowd had gathered. They watched breathlessly as the giant trudged closer to Balto, slowly pulling in the rope, while the horse kicked out his back legs in fury and tossed his head in a desperate attempt to free himself. His movements were so frantic, Beatrice was afraid he was going to hang himself. She flinched at the brutality of it. *Isn't there anything we can do to stop this?* she thought wildly. But she already knew the answer to that. If Balto was to be saved, he was going to have to do it himself.

Finally, the stallion stopped fighting. He stood motionless, breathing hard. Beatrice's heart sank as Balto slowly lowered his head to the ground, a gesture that seemed to acknowledge that his adversary had won.

The giant had stopped moving, as well. They couldn't see his expression from so far away, but the tilt of his head to the side suggested that Balto's submissive stance puzzled him.

Now that the horse was no longer struggling against his captor, the tension in the rope relaxed. Which must have been exactly what Balto had been counting on—because in the next moment, quick as a flash, the stallion slipped his head from the giant's lariat and reared up, pawing the air with his front hooves. Before the anxious crowd knew what was happening, Balto had spread his wings and was soaring skyward.

Beatrice heard startled gasps around her, and then screams of excitement. *Balto was free!*

Now everyone was clapping and chanting, "Balto! Balto! Balto!"

Beatrice noted with glee that the giant was standing in the same spot, shoulders slumped in dejection, the rope hanging loosely from his hands.

Meanwhile, the stallion made a wide sweep overhead and then turned back toward the ranch. He swooped down the side of Winged-Horse Mountain at an incredible speed, like a jet coming in for a landing. Then he leveled off, heading directly for the knot of people gathered in the ranch yard.

Witches started running in all directions.

"Duck!" Teddy shouted, and fell to the ground.

But Beatrice didn't move. She just stood there, staring, as if hypnotized by the streak of white speeding toward her.

And then, only seconds before he would have collided with her, the horse pulled up sharply. While the onlookers watched in astonishment, Balto soared toward the mountaintop.

Joy came back to stand with Beatrice, brushing sand from the front of her robes. "He heard you warn him," she said. "I believe he was thanking you."

"By nearly kicking my head in?" Beatrice asked, her voice shaking.

"By *not*," Joy replied, and started for the house.

Ira Skelly went trotting after her, and Beatrice and Teddy followed more slowly. Kasper fell into step with them.

"That was cool," he said. "I thought Balto was going to hit you."

"Yeah," Beatrice said dryly, "real cool."

After Dickens had seated Beatrice and her friends at a corner table, Beatrice checked out the room. There was Miranda, still disguised as Marco Bell in her white wig and beard, sitting at a table by herself. Uri Luna was with the campers, and Hyacinth Broomshead was sharing a table with Winifred Stoop. Beatrice noticed that the red-haired witch seemed to be talking poor Winifred's ear off. Then her attention drifted to Ira Skelly, who was happily ensconced at a table with Joy and Seamus. Beatrice smiled grimly. It was a relief to have him occupied elsewhere.

After Fairlamb had brought heaping plates of roasted lizard's tongue—with peanut butter and catmint jelly sandwiches for Cyrus—Beatrice said softly, "Let's talk about how we're going to reach the top of Blood Mountain."

"Uri offered to teach us to use the climbing equipment," Ollie said, "but I can't figure out how we'll be able to get past the Ghumbabas and the birds of prey."

Beatrice nodded. "I know. So I've been wondering if there might be a way to climb *inside* the mountain—you know, through the mine tunnels."

"Who could tell us?" Teddy asked.

No one answered because Fairlamb had returned with a basket of mosquito muffins and a second helping of lizard's tongue for Cayenne.

After the waitress had moved on to another table, Cyrus said, "Seamus might know if there's a way through the tunnels, but he's not likely to help us."

"And I hate to even mention Blood Mountain to Joy," Beatrice said. "It has to be a painful subject for her."

"Uri Luna grew up here," Ollie pointed out. "He'd probably know."

"But can we trust him?" Beatrice asked, watching idly as Cayenne speared a lizard's tongue with her claws and scarfed it down.

"I wouldn't trust any friend of Miranda's," Teddy responded.

Cyrus nodded vigorously as he bit into his third sandwich.

"Which brings up another question," Ollie said. "We agreed to let Miranda work with us, but just how much are we going to share with her? It could be dangerous to let her in on all our plans."

"*Very* dangerous," Teddy said emphatically. "She and Dally Rumpe could use anything we tell her to ambush us."

Just then, Beatrice noticed Dickens clearing dishes from a nearby table and an idea suddenly popped into her head.

"*The gnomes*," Beatrice said, her fork poised in midair. "Who knows the mine tunnels better than the miners?"

"That's brilliant!" Ollie exclaimed.

About that time, Beatrice realized that the dining room seemed unusually quiet. She glanced around and saw that quite a few eyes were focused on their table. Miranda was certainly looking at them, as were Hyacinth Broomshead and Uri Luna. But Beatrice was pretty sure they were too far away to have heard anything.

"Have you guys finished eating?" she asked. "I think we should continue our conversation upstairs."

Once they had closed the door to Beatrice and Teddy's room, Beatrice said, "I have an idea, but it's pretty wild."

"I think we could use a wild idea about now," Ollie said cheerfully. "Lay it on us."

Beatrice sank to the floor and the others gathered around her.

"Well," Beatrice said, "I was thinking that the gnomes would be able to tell us where the tunnels lead. But then I had another thought. What if we could go with them into the mines?"

Teddy gave her a dubious look. "Don't you think we'd kind of stand out? If nothing else, we're a whole lot taller than they are."

"But we could fix that," Cyrus said, grinning as he realized where Beatrice was going with this. "I could shrink us."

"But we still don't *look* like gnomes," Teddy protested. "They have beards and—" She stopped, a smile beginning to tug at her lips. "But we could wear fake beards, couldn't we? Like Miranda."

"And maybe Longfellow and Dickens could loan us some clothes," Ollie added.

Then Teddy's face fell. "But we'll need papers. Remember? Paxton said only gnomes with special papers were allowed in the mines."

Beatrice was thinking hard. The plan was too good to be abandoned so quickly. Besides, she couldn't figure out another way to get inside the mountain.

"We'll talk to Joy," Beatrice said. "Maybe Paxton can get us papers."

Even Ollie was looking uncertain now. "He didn't seem like the helpful type," Ollie said, "but we can try."

"And we'll ask Longfellow and Dickens to introduce us to their brothers and the other miners," Beatrice went on doggedly. "Surely *they* would want to help us overthrow Dally Rumpe."

"Okay," Ollie agreed. "Let's go talk to Joy first."

"She'll be busy tonight," Teddy said. "They're having a square dance for the guests."

"Well, *we're* guests," Cyrus said brightly. "So what are we waiting for?"

With a Western band playing beneath her window, and everyone doing do-si-dos across the patio under strings of twinkling lights, Beatrice was having a hard time keeping her mind on colonial America. She glanced at Cayenne, who was sitting at Beatrice's elbow peering down at the festivities.

"This is getting old," Beatrice grumbled to the cat. "You and I are missing out on *everything*."

Cayenne gave a sympathetic meow, but didn't look up from the activity outside their window.

Beatrice's eyes roamed over the crowd, picking out Teddy and Ollie, who were dancing together, and Cyrus, who was standing near the refreshments table stuffing his face. She saw Joy dancing with Ira, and Seamus steering a smiling Winifred gently around the dance floor.

"Everyone seems to be having fun," Beatrice said wistfully.

Well, not *everyone*, she amended, because she had just noticed a tall figure standing in the shadows on the other side of the pool, watching the dancers. Then Beatrice caught a glimpse of the hunter's bow, and knew that it was Orion.

What a strange guy, Beatrice thought. Why didn't he join the party instead of lurking around in the dark? Who was this mysterious witch, anyway, and what did he want?

"Maybe I should go talk to our mystery man," Beatrice said to Cayenne. "What do you think?"

The cat leaped to the floor and headed for the door.

"I see that you agree," Beatrice said, and closed her textbook.

Afraid that Ira would see her and demand to know why she wasn't working on her assignment, Beatrice avoided the patio, moving quickly around its shadowy perimeter. But when she reached the spot where Orion had been standing, she found that the hunter had disappeared.

Beatrice looked around, but there was no sign of Orion. She sighed and started back to the house. As she was circling the pool, she heard footsteps close behind her.

Beatrice spun around. She saw a dark shape looming over her and let out a yelp.

"Blesséd be," came a soft, familiar voice from out of the darkness. "What do you think I'm going to do, *strangle* you?"

It was only Miranda.

"I would appreciate it," Beatrice said tartly, "if you'd quit stalking me."

"I'll be glad to when you quit keeping secrets from me," Miranda snapped.

"What are you talking about?" Beatrice muttered as Miranda moved closer. "What secrets am I keeping?"

Miranda's face was partially hidden by the fake beard, but even in the dim light, there was no mistaking the displeasure in her expression. "I heard you and your dorky friends talking about posing as gnomes and going with them into the mines."

Beatrice's mouth fell open. "You were listening outside my room!"

"Don't look so scandalized," Miranda responded. "You said I could work with you—but you weren't about to let me in on your plans, were you?"

"I'd be more likely to if I thought I could trust you," Beatrice shot back, "but you don't give me much reason to."

They were glaring at each other, and Beatrice's heart was doing an indignant little dance.

"The point is, I heard everything," Miranda said. "Actually, it's not a bad idea. So I'll be going into the tunnels with you."

Beatrice opened her mouth to speak, but Miranda held up a hand to silence her. "Dally Rumpe told me that he lived for years in a cave inside Blood Mountain. He studied an old spellbook his father left him and prepared himself to take the kingdom of Bailiwick away from Bromwich."

Beatrice's eyes opened wide. "Do you know where the cave is?"

"I can find it," Miranda assured her. "And Dally Rumpe also told me that he left the spellbook in the cave. Who knows? *He* might even be there."

"I'd like to see that spellbook," Beatrice admitted. "If we can find the spell he cast on Bailiwick, it might help us reverse it."

"You see, Beatrice?" Miranda said, the old smugness creeping back into her voice. "You *do* need me."

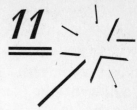

11

The Gnomes

While Ira was still occupied with Joy—stepping on her feet at regular intervals, Beatrice noticed, and grinning like he was trying out for a tooth-whitening ad—Beatrice managed to get her friends' attention and motioned for them to join her. When Teddy saw Miranda waiting with Beatrice, she bristled.

"What does *she* want?" Teddy demanded.

"She overheard us talking about going into the mines with the gnomes," Beatrice replied.

"You mean she had her ear pressed to the door," Teddy muttered.

"Do you mind not speaking about me as if I'm not here?" Miranda asked, narrowing her eyes at Teddy.

"Anyway," Beatrice went on, ignoring the tension between the two, "I think we might as well go ahead and talk to Longfellow and Dickens. That way, we'll know if the gnomes are going to help us before we mention it to Joy."

"I didn't see either Longfellow *or* Dickens at the dance," Ollie said.

"It's best if we catch them alone, anyway," Beatrice replied. "I wonder where they are."

"Right about now, they should be raiding the refrigerator," Miranda informed her. "They pig out every night till bedtime."

Sure enough, they found Longfellow and Dickens sitting at the kitchen table, surrounded by a large number of plastic containers. Each gnome had a plate heaped with food and was shoveling it in as fast as he could.

Longfellow looked up warily when Beatrice and her companions entered. Dickens grinned at them and continued to eat.

"Sorry to interrupt," Ollie said, "but we need to talk to you guys."

Dickens swallowed a mouthful and reached for another mosquito muffin. "Why don't you join us?" he said pleasantly. "There's plenty for everyone."

"Thanks," Beatrice said as she sat down across from the gnomes, "but we've already had dinner. We need to ask a favor."

Longfellow was eyeing them suspiciously, but his distrust didn't seem to affect his appetite. He speared a lizard's tongue and popped it into his mouth. Cayenne, who was staring transfixed from Beatrice's lap, began to drool.

"Okay, it's like this," Beatrice said to the gnomes. "We're here to try to break Dally Rumpe's spell on Blood Mountain, but in order to do that, we need to reach the top of the mountain."

"Only the Ghumbabas and the birds of prey are going to make that difficult," Teddy added, "so we were wondering—"

Miranda made an impatient sound in her throat and slapped her palm down on the table. Everyone jumped. Longfellow glowered.

"Let's stop beating around the bush," Miranda said brusquely. "We want to go into the mines with the gnomes. And you have to help us."

Longfellow and Dickens's eyebrows shot up and they exchanged a look. Then Dickens began to giggle, and Longfellow looked grouchier than ever.

"Only gnomes are allowed in the mines," Longfellow said gruffly.

"Besides," Dickens added blithely, "the Ghumbaba on guard would have to think you're a gnome, and you're *way* too tall."

"That's no problem," Ollie said. "We can shrink ourselves down to your size. And if you'd let us borrow some of your clothes—"

"—and help us with beards and stuff—" Cyrus said.

Longfellow and Dickens glanced at each other again, and said nothing.

"Your brothers work in the mines, don't they?" Beatrice asked the gnomes. When they nodded, she said, "And working for Dally Rumpe can't be easy for them. But with your help, we might be able to change that. Wouldn't the miners be happy to see Dally Rumpe gone?"

"They certainly would," Dickens replied fervently, and even Longfellow was forced to agree.

"Then will you help us get inside the tunnels?" Ollie asked hopefully.

Dickens turned to his brother. "I think we have to, Bubba."

Longfellow's scowl showed how hard he was resisting, but finally he said grudgingly, "Let's see what Chaucer and O. Henry have to say about it."

We're making progress, Beatrice thought, and she and her friends looked more hopeful. Less patient, Miranda rolled her eyes as if to say, *Can't we just get on with it?*

"May we go with you to see Chaucer and O. Henry?" Beatrice asked.

"If you really think it's necessary," Longfellow grumbled, "but you can't go lumbering into the village with those big feet. You might squash somebody."

"No problem," Cyrus said. "Everybody stand up and hold hands."

The gnomes watched with interest as Cyrus began to murmur the words to the shrinking spell, and then blinked in amazement when the five witches began to grow smaller and smaller.

"Now that's more like it," Dickens said. He sidled over to a two-foot Ollie and poked him playfully in the ribs. "But you're a little skinny for a gnome."

"It's getting late," Longfellow said, jumping down from his chair. "Come on if you're going with us."

As they walked across the dark expanse of desert toward Winged-Horse Mountain, Beatrice couldn't even see the gnome village. Then they entered the scraggly growth at the base of the mountain, and dozens of tiny, brightly lit windows came into view. As they moved closer, Beatrice heard lively fiddle music and the laughter of gnomes having a good time.

They followed a path that wound over a hillock of sand and then down into the village. A cluster of cottages nestled comfortably in the shadows against the side of the mountain.

Longfellow walked up to one of the cottages and rapped on the door. The music and laughter stopped abruptly, and the door slowly opened. A gnome with a beard almost as long as Longfellow's peeked out cautiously. Then his face relaxed and he yelled over his shoulder, "It's Longfellow and Dickens! And—some other creatures."

"This is my brother, O. Henry," Longfellow said.

O. Henry was peering at Beatrice and her friends with a puzzled expression. "Elves?" he asked Longfellow.

"Witches," Longfellow replied, frowning in Beatrice's direction. "They can shrink themselves."

Now O. Henry appeared fearful. "They're not Dally Rumpe's people," he said hastily.

"No, no," Dickens said, stepping up to the door. "In fact, they've come to try to break Dally Rumpe's spell. This is Beatrice Bailey, Henry. You've heard of her."

O. Henry nodded, still looking uncertain. "Hmmm," he said. "Well, come in, all of you. Some of our neighbors are here. And Chaucer and his family," he added to Longfellow and Dickens.

They filed through the door into a room with white-washed walls and a tiled floor. Candles flickered on every surface, and dried herbs hung from the low ceiling rafters. Several gnomes were seated at a table—piled high, pre-dictably, with food—while others were gathered around a gnome holding a fiddle. A few young gnomes were playing with toys on the floor. Everyone was looking at Beatrice and her companions with a mixture of curiosity and trepidation. Then a full-size Cayenne came sauntering in, and there was an audible gasp.

"What is *that?*" a fair-haired woman exclaimed, and grabbed for a round-faced baby at her feet.

"This is my cat-familiar," Beatrice said hastily. "She's very gentle. You have nothing to worry about, really."

An older woman with gray braids wrapped around her head was still frowning at Cayenne. "That black cat from the ranch has been known to pounce on us. We can't let the children play outside without supervision."

"Cayenne doesn't pounce on people," Beatrice said firmly. "She wouldn't hurt a fly."

"All right then," the woman said, her face relaxing a little. "Come in and have something to eat. I'm O. Henry's wife, Marietta, by the way. If you're friends of Longfellow and Dickens, you're always welcome here."

It seemed to Beatrice that the gnomes' favorite pastime was eating, and Marietta insisted that everyone fill his or her plate—several times—before any business was discussed. It wasn't until the last morsel of food was gone that the gnomes sat back with sighs of satisfaction and waited for Longfellow to speak.

Beatrice and her companions sat quietly while Longfellow explained that they needed the gnomes' help.

"But only gnomes can go into the mines," one of the men said when Longfellow was finished.

"Who made that rule, anyway?" another one asked.

"It must have been Dally Rumpe," a third man said with a scowl. "Because back in Bromwich's time, after the new tunnels were opened, we had witches helping out for a while."

"Then there's no gnome law that says these witches can't go with us," O. Henry said thoughtfully.

"And they *are* trying to help us," Marietta pointed out.

"We'll vote on it," Chaucer said, and turned to Beatrice. "You and your friends will have to step outside. Gnome votes are taken in secret."

Longfellow held the door open for them.

"This is a waste of time," Miranda grumbled as the door closed in her face. "We don't need their permission to go into the tunnels."

"Actually, we do," Beatrice replied. "They're going to have to accept us and treat us like one of them. Otherwise, the Ghumbabas will know something's wrong."

A long time passed. Beatrice could hear the murmur of voices—and sometimes, the raised voice of a passionate gnome making a point. She was beginning to think they would never reach a decision when the door suddenly opened.

"Come in," Longfellow said.

Once inside, Beatrice saw that the gnomes appeared very solemn. This didn't look promising. It was O. Henry who stood up to address them.

"We've talked at length about what we should do in this matter," he said to Beatrice and her companions, "which led to a lot of reminiscing about the old times." He sighed, looking as sad as a gnome can look. "It was different when Bromwich was here. He wouldn't have let anyone treat us badly, and we had reasonable work hours and good salaries. Now we mine seven days a week, and we aren't paid enough to keep our children in shoes."

Beatrice noticed that some of the gnomes had tears in their eyes, and others looked angry.

"Beatrice Bailey," O. Henry continued, "you are the first witch to come here and say you want to help us. We don't have a lot of hope that you'll succeed," he admitted, looking at her shyly with a hint of apology in his voice, "but to even try is a noble gesture. Therefore, we have voted unanimously to help you in any way we can."

Beatrice was thrilled! But then she looked around at the faces of the miners and their families and saw that they were weighted down with the weariness that comes from a long, terrible struggle. Beatrice's elation was tempered by the knowledge that her success or failure would mean everything to these gnomes. Whether their futures were grim or hopeful depended entirely on her.

Feeling both humble and anxious, Beatrice squared her shoulders and blew her bangs out of her eyes. "Thank you," she said. "I can't promise that we'll be able to break Dally Rumpe's spell, but we're going to try very hard. We don't want to let you down."

With these words, the gnomes' expressions softened. Even Longfellow looked almost friendly.

"You'll need clothes," Marietta said briskly, and lifting the top of a dome-lid trunk, she began to pull out shirts and trousers.

"And hard hats," Chaucer said.

"And we'll have to fix them up with beards," O. Henry added.

"Ladies, can you spare some of your wigs?" Marietta asked, sounding almost excited as she looked around the room. "They could be used to make fine beards."

Suddenly all the women were rushing out the door, coming back in a short time with wigs, hard hats, socks, and boots. Meanwhile, Chaucer had begun to draw a map of the mines.

"Here's the entrance," he said, pointing to the drawing. "You can see that the main tunnel goes straight back, with several smaller ones branching off of it. Now this back tunnel goes up toward the top of the mountain, but we haven't mined that part yet, so I don't know how far it goes. I did hear rumors that they were going to make another entrance at the top. Whether they have or not, I can't say."

"We'll have to go in and see," Beatrice replied. She glanced up from the map at Miranda. "Where would Dally Rumpe's cave be?" she asked.

A secretive smile played across Miranda's lips. "I'll show you once we're inside," she answered.

Teddy's expression said plainly that she would like nothing better than to punch Miranda's lights out.

Chaucer was still bent over the table, studying the map. Then he looked up abruptly. "I nearly forgot. You'll need identification papers. But the only one who can get you those is Paxton Rowntree."

"Does he make them up himself?" Beatrice asked.

Chaucer nodded. "He has these forms, and all he has to do is fill in names and dates of employment, that sort of thing."

"Will he help us?" Ollie asked.

No one spoke for a moment. Then O. Henry said with a slight frown, "Paxton's okay. He does as much for us as he can—a *lot* more than the last foreman. But he still works for Dally Rumpe, doesn't he?" The gnome shrugged. "I don't know if he'll help you or not."

The square dance was still in full swing when Beatrice and her friends returned to the ranch. Cyrus made them all big again so that they could join the other guests for refreshments. As she sipped a glass of phantom punch, Beatrice noticed that Joy was dancing with Uri, leaving Fairlamb and Ira to mope on the sidelines.

Beatrice slipped behind a cluster of people so that Ira wouldn't see her. But just then, Hyacinth Broomshead yelled out her name from across the patio, effectively destroying Beatrice's hope for anonymity. The red-haired witch elbowed her way through the dancers, not seeming to notice their scowls in her direction, and sashayed up to Beatrice.

"I've been looking everywhere for you!" Hyacinth exclaimed, slipping her arm around Beatrice's shoulder as if they were old friends. "I'd just love to hear your plans for breaking the spell on Winged-Horse Mountain."

"Our plans are vague at the moment," Beatrice replied, edging away from Hyacinth's embrace.

Hyacinth's eyes narrowed. "Cagey, aren't we?" the older witch murmured.

Then Hyacinth began to pluck at something on Beatrice's shoulder, like she was picking off lint.

Beatrice had had enough. She pulled back from the woman, noticeably irritated, and said, "You'll have to excuse me. It's been a long day and I need to get some sleep."

Hyacinth pursed her lips, but then she smiled and said, "Of course, dearie. But you have to promise to keep me up on things. I'm a big fan, you know."

"A *big* fan," Ollie whispered with a grin as they started for the house.

Beatrice sighed. She was just glad to get away from the obnoxious witch. And she *was* tired. Her bed was going to feel really good tonight. But then she saw Winifred Stoop coming toward them.

"Are you children calling it an evening?" Winifred asked. "I think I should, too," she added with a twinkle in her eyes. "I haven't danced this much in forty years, and my feet are killing me."

"We'll go with you," Beatrice said, and took the older witch's arm.

Everyone else was still outside when they entered the ranch house.

"I couldn't help noticing that Hyacinth Broomshead had you cornered again," Winifred said as they started up the stairs. "You wouldn't happen to be missing anything, would you?"

Beatrice turned a surprised face to Winifred. "No, I don't think so," she replied.

"What about your watch?" Winifred asked, giving Beatrice a shrewd look.

"That's right—I have misplaced it," Beatrice said quickly. "How did you know?"

"Because I think I saw Hyacinth slip it off your wrist at dinner one night," Winifred replied calmly. "Are you missing anything else?"

"A hair clip," Beatrice said. "But why would Hyacinth want that?"

Winifred's sharp eyes bore into Beatrice's face. "Why would she want some of your hair?" Seeing Beatrice's bewildered expression, Winifred said, "I noticed her picking loose hairs off your shoulder a moment ago, and then slipping them into her pocket."

Looking as perplexed as Beatrice, Teddy said, "What possible use could Hyacinth have for Beatrice's hair?"

"I can't be certain," Winifred said thoughtfully, "but witches who practice dark magic sometimes use their victim's hair or nail clippings on wax dolls they make in the victim's image."

Ollie and Cyrus were staring at Winifred in horror.

"They stick pins in the dolls!" Teddy exclaimed.

"Or burn them," Winifred said. "Anything that would harm the victim."

Despite the warmth of the night, Beatrice suddenly felt cold. "Then you think Hyacinth practices dark magic and is out to get me?" she asked hoarsely.

"I don't know," Winifred admitted, frowning. "But her actions are odd, wouldn't you agree?"

Very *odd*, Beatrice thought. Could it be that Hyacinth was working for Dally Rumpe? Beatrice didn't have any enemies that she knew of besides the evil sorcerer, so anything suspicious always seemed to come back to him.

Winifred was watching Beatrice closely. "The bad omens I mentioned to you," she said softly, "did they come to pass? Three people plotting? A falling star?"

Beatrice was feeling shaky. She took a deep breath and blew her bangs out of her eyes. "They did," she replied, and a sense of dread settled over her like a heavy blanket.

"Then you must be especially careful," Winifred said gently. "And watch out for Hyacinth Broomshead. Whatever she's up to, I can guarantee you that it's not good."

12

Phantom Rodeo

The next morning, when Ollie and Cyrus met the girls for breakfast, Ollie said to Beatrice, "We have to confront Hyacinth."

"I agree," Teddy said promptly. "I dreamed about little wax dolls with pins sticking out of them all night long."

Beatrice groaned. She hadn't slept well, herself, and there was still the unfinished history assignment hanging over her head. All in all, things didn't seem to be going her way—and the last thing she needed was a close encounter with someone who wanted to put a curse on her.

"Where's Ira?" Beatrice asked as they started down the stairs.

Ollie grinned and shook his head. "He was gone before Cyrus and I got up—off to pester his lady love to death, no doubt."

Teddy grimaced. "Can you imagine having someone like Ira Skelly in love with you? Yuck!"

"Look, there's Hyacinth now," Ollie said as they reached the bottom of the stairs.

Beatrice looked up, and sure enough, the red-haired witch was crossing the lobby toward the dining room.

"Hyacinth!" Teddy called.

The older witch turned and her face lit up when she saw Beatrice.

"How perfect," Hyacinth gushed, running over to meet them. "We can have breakfast together."

"Actually," Ollie said, "we need to talk to you in private."

Looking suddenly wary, Hyacinth hesitated, then followed Ollie and the others to a conversation area in the corner.

"Please, sit down," Ollie said to Hyacinth.

Hyacinth plopped down into an overstuffed chair. "What is this all about?" she asked, sounding vaguely alarmed. "Is there a problem?"

"Maybe you can help us figure that out," Ollie replied.

Beatrice and Cyrus sat down on the couch beside Teddy, and Ollie perched on the arm of a chair. They were all looking at Hyacinth, who was visibly nervous. Beatrice thought the woman's face was turning red—but it was hard to be sure with that ton of makeup she wore.

"We know what you've been doing," Ollie said, his voice very stern.

"Doing? I'm sure I don't know what you're talking about," Hyacinth said, plucking anxiously at the skirt of her robes.

"You've been stealing from Beatrice!" Cyrus burst out. "You took her watch—and her hair!"

Hyacinth sank back weakly into the chair. "I don't steal," she murmured faintly. "You have no proof."

"Oh, but we do," Ollie said evenly. "We have a witness."

Hyacinth's eyes opened wide. Then she heaved a sigh. "All right," she said, "you've found me out."

Beatrice blinked in surprise. She hadn't expected the witch to admit so readily to being a thief.

"You took my watch," Beatrice said, "and a hair clip."

"Well—yes. And a few of your hairs," Hyacinth added. "Oh, and a napkin you used at dinner one night."

"*What?*" Beatrice stared at the woman in disbelief. "What could you have possibly wanted with my napkin?"

Hyacinth pulled a handkerchief from her pocket and began to dab at her eyes. "I was going to—to—"

"Yes?" Teddy prompted impatiently. "What were you going to do?"

"Sell the stuff at an online auction site," Hyacinth blurted out. "There's Beatrice Bailiwick memorabilia all over the Witch World Web—probably most of it fake."

That's a safe bet, Beatrice thought in bewilderment. She didn't think she had any teeth or underwear missing.

"But all mine is real," Hyacinth said, giving them a watery smile. "Beatrice Bailiwick's watch. A napkin that Beatrice Bailiwick used to wipe her lips. Beatrice Bailiwick's *hair!*"

"We get the idea," Ollie broke in hastily.

"It wasn't really stealing," Hyacinth said defensively. "Nothing I took is valuable. Even the watch is cheap."

Beatrice bristled at that.

"But collectors will pay a fortune for this junk," Hyacinth went on. "And I need money. The Broomshead fortune is long gone."

Teddy was regarding her with disgust. "Have you done anything like this before, or is Beatrice your first victim?"

"I've taken an item or two in the past," Hyacinth admitted reluctantly. "Celebrity memorabilia is always in demand."

"I think I'm beginning to see," Ollie said, looking none too happy. "You travel around to resorts where you know famous people are going to be and take things from them to sell."

Hyacinth frowned. "You make it sound *easy*. Well, let me tell you, it's *not*. Celebrities protect their privacy like crazy, especially when they're on vacation. I have to really work to track them down." Then she turned to Beatrice and smiled. "I just missed you at Sea-Dragon Bay."

Beatrice didn't care to hear any more. "I want my watch back," she said, "and my hair clip."

"And don't forget the napkin," Cyrus added, his expression fierce. Then to Beatrice he whispered, "You don't want her to have anything with your DNA on it."

"Let's go up to your room right now," Teddy said, already getting up from the couch.

Hyacinth's shoulders slumped. "That won't be necessary," she said mournfully. "I keep all my merchandise with me."

Beatrice watched as the witch dug around in her tote bag, producing Beatrice's watch, her hair clip, and finally, a white cloth napkin.

Beatrice grabbed for the stuff, feeling a little sick.

"You aren't going to have me arrested, are you?" Hyacinth asked, adopting a timid voice that was completely out of character.

"We should," Ollie answered gruffly. "You'll just go on doing this till you're caught."

"Actually, I've already decided to give it up," Hyacinth said. "You probably think rubbing shoulders with celebrities would be exciting, but it isn't. They're unbelievably spoiled and stupid."

Beatrice cut her eyes at the woman and Teddy giggled.

Ollie was trying not to grin. "Well, what do you think, Beatrice?" he asked.

Beatrice gave Hyacinth a hard look. "Promise me that you won't ever steal again," she said.

Hyacinth was noticeably relieved. "Oh, I won't. You can count on it." She sighed as if a major burden had been lifted, and added, "I'm so glad you understand, dearie."

They watched as she headed for the dining room, appearing very pleased with herself. Something told Beatrice that Hyacinth would be making reservations at her next resort before the day was over.

"Well, now that that's settled," Cyrus said, "let's go eat. I'm starving!"

But before they reached the dining room, Seamus Griffin came striding in, his eyes filled with fury.

Ollie was about to say good morning, but Seamus cut him off.

"I've been looking for you," the ranch owner said to Beatrice, practically spitting out the words. "It's come to my attention that you've had a secret meeting with the gnomes. And I think I have a pretty good idea why. You think they'll help you gain access to that mountain!"

Seamus's anger was so intense, Beatrice took a step back.

"Well?" the man demanded. "What do you have to say for yourself?"

Ollie came to stand beside Beatrice and said calmly to Seamus, "I didn't realize the gnome village was off limits. Maybe you should post a sign."

Seamus gave Ollie a piercing look. "Smart mouth you have there," he muttered, then his eyes shifted back to Beatrice. "I told you when you arrived that you aren't welcome here. I won't be a party to you all getting yourselves killed!"

"We heard about your son," Beatrice said gently. "We're very sorry."

Seamus's face registered shock, then desperate unhappiness.

"I understand why you're so against us going to Blood Mountain," Beatrice went on, "but I don't have a choice. The Bailiwicks are my family, and Morven is up on that mountain waiting for someone to help her. I have to try, Mr. Griffin."

All of Seamus's fury had drained away. He looked deflated.

"Dominy was a good boy," Seamus said, his voice barely above a whisper. "Never gave me any trouble. I don't know what got into him—why he'd do such a foolish thing."

Teddy patted Seamus's arm awkwardly, and Cyrus and Ollie moved closer to him, but no one knew what to say. What can you say to a man who's lost his only son?

Seamus took a deep shaky breath. Then he raised his eyes to Beatrice's face.

"You're good kids, too," he said wearily. "I don't want your families going through what I have. And Joy. They were going to be married, you know. Her life is ruined."

"We'll be careful," Beatrice promised.

Seamus just shook his head sadly. "There's no way to be careful on that mountain. No one can survive it."

After breakfast, they went looking for Joy and found her stocking shelves in the pantry. Beatrice tried to ease into the topic of Blood Mountain, but as soon as she mentioned needing papers from Paxton, Joy's eyes flashed with alarm.

"No," Joy said, shaking her head vehemently. "It's too dangerous, for you *and* for Paxton. If Dally Rumpe found out—*No!* I won't ask him."

"Okay," Beatrice said. She was disappointed, but she wasn't going to try to change Joy's mind. "We understand. We'll ask Paxton ourselves."

"Don't you get it?" Joy demanded. "If you set foot on that mountain, you won't come back. Period! No one has *ever* come back."

"Uri told us about Dominy," Beatrice said, "and we don't want to make it harder for you, but if we just take off by ourselves, we know we won't make it. Our only hope is to go with the gnomes. Maybe then we'll have a chance."

Joy looked as if she couldn't decide whether to plead with Beatrice or scream at her. Finally, running her fingers through her sun-streaked hair in a gesture of frustration, she said, "All *right!* I'll talk to Paxton."

"I hadn't thought about us putting Paxton at risk," Beatrice admitted. "I wish we didn't have to involve him."

"He's *already* involved," Joy said heavily. "He blames himself for Dominy's death. I've tried to get him to see that they were just kids, that his teasing isn't what made Dominy climb that mountain—no matter what Uri Luna thinks! But Paxton won't listen to reason." She paused, looking uncertain. "If Paxton helps you, and you're able to break the spell, maybe he'll feel less guilty and be able to get on with his life."

Joy reached into the pocket of her robes and withdrew a photograph. Its corners were bent and she tried to smooth them with her hand.

"Is that Dominy?" Beatrice asked, staring down into the good-natured face of a handsome young man.

Not looking up from the photo, Joy nodded. "This was taken a few weeks before he died. On his twenty-second birthday." Her eyes filled with tears as she caressed the smiling face with her thumb.

Then she straightened up and blinked away the tears. "See the medallion he's wearing?" she asked.

Beatrice's eyes fell on the circle of gold hanging from a chain around Dominy's neck.

"That was my birthday present to him," Joy said. "It had a ruby in the center."

Beatrice peered closer at the medallion. "Did the ruby come from the Blood Mountain mines?"

"Yes, a long time ago," Joy replied. "The medallion had been passed down in my family for generations. I thought," she added, her voice quivering, "that Dominy would give it to *our* child one day. But it's lost now— somewhere on that mountain."

When Beatrice and her friends came out from the kitchen, they saw that the lobby was packed with people. Ollie punched her arm and pointed to the front desk, where Hyacinth Broomshead was paying her bill.

"Thank goodness she's leaving," Beatrice said in relief. "But what's everyone else doing here?"

"Haven't you noticed the flyers posted all over the place?" Cyrus asked. "The Phantom Rodeo's today."

"Why don't we go?" Ollie suggested. "We can't do anything about breaking Dally Rumpe's spell till we hear from Paxton, anyway."

"It *would* be fun," Beatrice said. Then her face fell. "But I have studying to do. And speaking of that, there's Ira," she added, ducking quickly behind Ollie and Teddy.

"He's heading for the kitchen," Teddy said, "so you know he'll be staying here with Joy. Come on, Beatrice. You'll have all afternoon to work on your assignment."

"I guess we shouldn't miss the rodeo," Beatrice said. Then she saw Winifred Stoop, wearing a ten-gallon Stetson and a red bandana around her neck, waving at them. "Come on, let's go with Winifred. She can explain everything to us."

An old blue bus with peeling paint and rusted hub-caps pulled up as everyone came pouring out of the ranch house. Beatrice had expected something magical—like flying horses, maybe—to transport them to the rodeo, not this old clunker.

The thought of flying horses made Beatrice look around for Balto. And there he was, standing on the highest peak of Winged-Horse Mountain, with one foreleg raised in the air. He seemed to be looking directly at her as he lowered his hoof slowly to the ground and pawed—but too gently to create thunder and lightning.

Beatrice took a step toward him. She could feel a connection between them, almost like an electric current passing from her eyes to his. She suspected that Balto was sending her a message—telling her that he could start a fire anytime he wanted, and he wasn't *about* to be bested by a puny witch like her.

The horse pawed the earth again. Beatrice looked steadily at him, feeling their connection strengthen. Then, suddenly, Balto reared up and beat the air with his front hooves. Seconds later, he was soaring through the sky toward Blood Mountain.

"What a beauty," Teddy murmured, and Beatrice nodded.

"He hasn't been starting fires since you put the last one out," Ollie said. "I think maybe you're taming him."

"Never," Beatrice said, squinting against the red glow as she watched Balto circle Blood Mountain. "I wouldn't want to."

Someone pushed Beatrice toward the bus, bringing her out of her reverie. She climbed the steps and found a seat about halfway back. Cayenne leaped to her shoulder and Ollie sat down beside her. Teddy and Cyrus took the seat behind them. Then Beatrice saw Uri boarding, with Miranda—still masquerading as Marco Bell—right behind him. Uri turned around and said something to Miranda, and they both laughed.

Teddy leaned forward and whispered to Beatrice, "I still don't trust those two."

"Neither do I," Beatrice replied.

Miranda paused when she reached Beatrice's seat.

"Have you talked to Joy?" she asked in a low voice.

Beatrice figured that the less her cousin knew, the better, but she wasn't going to lie. "A few minutes ago."

"And?" Miranda prompted.

"She's going to talk to Paxton."

"Well, keep me informed," Miranda said, making it sound like an order, and swished down the aisle after Uri.

The bus started off with a bang and a sputter, and soon they were rolling through the ranch gates and out across the desert at an amazing speed.

"That driver must have never heard of a straight line," Ollie said, looking queasy as the bus careened first to the left and then to the right.

Beatrice grinned, enjoying the roller-coaster effect, and glanced up front to see who was driving the bus. She saw with a shock that no one was. The driver's seat was empty!

"This bus is magic," Beatrice murmured.

"What did you say?" Ollie asked weakly, gripping the seat in front of him.

"I was telling you to take deep breaths," Beatrice said. "That's right. We should be there before long."

And so they were. A few minutes later, the blue bus rattled to a stop in front of a complex of stables and fenced paddocks. Mobs of people were already there, many of them wearing cowboy hats and boots.

A group of campers followed Beatrice and her friends off the bus, and Kasper fell into step beside Beatrice.

"Isn't this great?" the young witch said, his dark eyes sparkling with excitement. "I've never been to a rodeo before."

"Then you're in for a treat, young man," Winifred Stoop said as she hobbled over to join them.

They merged into the stream of people entering the complex, going down a long enclosed ramp and then into a bleacher area that encircled a large fenced corral.

"Let's sit over here," Winifred said. "We'll have a good view of the cowboys and their horses when they come in."

Beatrice sat down next to Winifred, with Kasper on her other side. Cayenne jumped into Beatrice's lap and sniffed the air—which even to Beatrice's nose smelled strongly of horses. Teddy, Ollie, and Cyrus found seats directly below them.

Cyrus caught sight of a young man selling refreshments and started waving his arm.

Teddy peered at Cyrus over the top of her glasses. "How can you be hungry already? We had a late breakfast."

"Fresh air always gives me an appetite," Cyrus answered primly.

"*Breathing* gives you an appetite," Teddy said.

But Cyrus wasn't to be deterred. He was soon wolfing down a bedbug burger, fury fries, and a bottle of rodeo root beer.

"Oh, here they come," Winifred said, her voice a little breathless.

Beatrice craned to see the parade of cowboys on horseback that was entering the corral. Animals and riders were all decked out in colorful costumes and tack, hardly looking like ghosts at all except that their outlines were a little blurred and wispy.

"There he is," Winifred said suddenly. She stood up and started to wave. "Hector!" she shouted. "Hector Stoop!"

Beatrice noticed one of the riders turning in his saddle and looking in their direction. When he saw Winifred, a big smile spread across his face and he raised his hat to her. Then he blew her a kiss. Beatrice was startled by how young he looked, until she remembered that Hector Stoop had been dead for forty years.

"Wow," Kasper said in an awed voice. "Will you look at them? I wish I could be a cowboy."

"You can be anything you want to be," Beatrice answered.

The boy's wistful eyes stayed glued on the horses and riders. "No, I can't," he said. "I'll be whatever my father wants me to be."

The parade circled the corral to thunderous applause, and to Winifred's surprisingly loud screams. An announcer was telling the crowd that the bronco riders would be up first.

"That's when the cowboy tries to stay in the saddle while his horse tries even harder to buck him off," Winifred explained to Beatrice, and then starting waving wildly again as her Hector was leaving the arena.

Beatrice wasn't sure she wanted to see some poor cowboy thrown and trampled, even if ghosts didn't bleed.

Winifred had sat back down, her cheeks flushed and her eyes bright.

"I nearly forgot to ask you," she said to Beatrice. "Did you get your things back from Hyacinth? Your watch and the hairs she took?"

"Yes, I—" Beatrice started to answer, then stopped short. The *hairs!* She didn't get the hairs.

The first bronco rider had come bucking into the arena, but Beatrice barely noticed him. All she could think about was Hyacinth Broomshead. Had that wily witch really meant to sell her things online, or was that just a smoke screen for more sinister intentions?

Beatrice couldn't shake the terrible feeling that Hyacinth was a lot more clever—and evil?—than they had given her credit for.

13

A Midnight Ride

eatrice and the others piled off the bus and hurried into the ranch house, eager for a cold drink after their hot, dusty ride across the desert. Joy had set up a table with iced phantom punch in the lobby.

"This is good," Beatrice and Teddy said at the same time.

Cyrus and Ollie were too intent on gulping down their punch to comment.

"It's about time you got back!" came an angry voice from behind them.

A startled Beatrice jumped, but she recognized the voice and her heart sank. She turned around and found herself eyeball-to-eyeball with a glaring Ira Skelly.

"Your assignment is way overdue," he snapped. "At this rate, we won't get past Chapter 5 before it's time for you to go home."

"Well," Beatrice said, angry herself now, but also feeling like a little kid who'd been caught skipping school, "I've been rather busy."

Ira snorted. "So I see. Watching a bunch of ghouls rope calves is certainly more important than your academic career."

Beatrice's face flooded with color. She was about to tell Ira to get off her back, but Ollie spoke first.

"It's like this," Ollie said calmly to Ira. "Dr. Featherstone asked you to tutor Beatrice, not be her jailer. She's come here on a very important—not to mention, dangerous!—mission, so who can blame her for not being able to concentrate on American history?"

"The fact remains," Ira said, glowering at Ollie, "that we both have a job to do, and *she's* making it impossible for me to do mine."

"Then why don't you quit?" Beatrice demanded. Seeing the gratifying look of surprise on Ira's face, she added, "Yeah, just *quit!*"

Ollie turned to Beatrice. "You aren't going to get any meaningful studying done while we're here, so why don't you stop torturing yourself with deadlines? Read what you can, and when we get home, *I'll* help you. I've never studied mortal history, but I can read! We'll get you ready for the makeup exam, I promise."

Beatrice and Ira's eyes were glued to Ollie. Beatrice was positively beaming, while Ira's mouth hung open as if he couldn't believe what he had just heard.

"You mean," Ira said incredulously, "that you don't want my help?"

Cyrus sauntered up to Ira. "That's right, oh, brilliant tutor," he said sassily, "so why don't you buzz off?"

His eyes blazing, Ira said, "Well, we'll just see about this. I'm going to send a message to Dr. Featherstone immediately!"

Beatrice was beginning to worry as she watched Ira stomp off. "I wish he wouldn't get Dr. Featherstone involved," she said.

"Don't let it bother you," Ollie replied. "Dr. F just came up with this tutoring idea so you could come back to the Sphere."

"That's right," Teddy said. "She doesn't give a flip whether you pass the history exam or not."

Beatrice took a deep breath and blew her bangs out of her eyes. "I guess you're right," she said. Then she looked shyly at Ollie. "Thanks for offering to help me."

Ollie smiled, looking pleased and a little embarrassed. "I can't think of anything I'd rather do," he replied.

Just then, Beatrice caught sight of Joy and Paxton coming in from the patio. Joy saw Beatrice and started toward her, with a noticeably reluctant Paxton trailing behind.

"Did you enjoy the rodeo?" Joy asked Beatrice and her friends.

They all assured her that the morning had been a lot of fun.

Beatrice was watching Paxton, but he was staring at the floor, refusing to meet her gaze. *This doesn't look good,* Beatrice thought. *He isn't going to help us.*

"Well, do you want to tell them?" Joy asked, glancing at her brother.

Paxton looked up, frowning. "Joy mentioned what you're planning to do," he said gruffly, his eyebrows pinched together in disapproval, "and I don't mind telling you that it's the stupidest idea I've ever heard. There's no way you're going to get away with impersonating gnomes."

"I can shrink us," Cyrus began, but Paxton raised a hand to silence him.

"It's not your size," Paxton said, "it's your—*presence.* Gnomes have a different attitude than witches do."

"Attitude is one thing I have plenty of," Teddy informed Paxton. "I'll be a better gnome than most of the *gnomes!*"

For a moment, Beatrice thought that Paxton was actually going to smile, but then he seemed to catch himself and looked grumpier than ever.

Beatrice sighed. "So you aren't going to help us."

"Paxton," Joy said softly, looking steadily at her brother.

He let out a frustrated breath. "My sister thinks I should," Paxton said grudgingly. "I disagree, but Joy has always been able to convince me of things against my better judgment."

Beatrice's eyes lit up, and she couldn't control the grin spreading across her face. "Than you'll get us the papers?"

Paxton's frown deepened. He reached into a breast pocket inside his robes, removed a stack of folded papers, and held them out to Beatrice.

She unfolded the top sheet and read softly, "*Name: Curlicue Jingles. Species: Gnome. Occupation: Miner. Assignment: Blood Mountain Ruby Mines.*"

Beatrice looked up at Paxton. "Thank you," she said simply.

"There are papers for five, as you requested," Paxton said. "So who's going to use the fifth ID?"

"That's just in case someone else decides to go with us," Beatrice answered lamely.

"I didn't think you'd want Cayenne to go," Joy said, glancing at the cat on Beatrice's shoulder. "She has plenty of attitude, but even those giants aren't stupid enough to believe that *she's* a gnome. I'll take care of her, if you like."

"That would be great," Beatrice replied.

Cayenne, however, didn't seem pleased with the arrangement. She was swishing her tail angrily and peering at Joy through narrow green-gold slits.

"Cayenne has saved us more than once," Beatrice said as she stroked the cat. "She led us through enchanted fog at Werewolf Close and saved me from an army of vicious rats at Sea-Dragon Bay. I think she's unhappy about being left behind this time."

Joy reached out to pet the cat, and Cayenne allowed it, although she was still glaring. "You just don't look the part," Joy said gently to Cayenne. "You're far too beautiful. If you stay here with me, I'll cook you something special. How about a thick bat steak?"

Cayenne's tail slowed and then she bumped her head affectionately against Joy's hand. When the cat started to purr, Beatrice grinned at Joy.

"I think you have a new best friend," Beatrice said.

"So when are we going into the mines?" Cyrus asked.

Beatrice looked at Ollie and then Teddy. "Tomorrow morning? We should leave as soon as possible, don't you think?"

Ollie nodded, and Teddy said, "The longer we wait, the more likely someone will find out what we're planning."

"We appreciate your help," Ollie said to Paxton. "Can you tell the gnomes to expect us in the morning?"

Paxton just nodded, seeming more worried now than angry. "There are bones all over that mountain," he said quietly, "all that remains of good witches who thought they could win out over Dally Rumpe."

Joy's face went pale. "Paxton, don't," she said. "It isn't your fault that Dominy—"

Paxton's eyes were suddenly filled with anguish. "It *is* my fault! If I hadn't hounded him when we were kids, he wouldn't have felt he had to prove himself. But I never meant . . ." His voice trailed off, and he turned accusing eyes on Beatrice. "If something happens to you, I'll have that on my conscience, as well."

After Joy and Paxton had left, Beatrice and her friends started upstairs. Beatrice wasn't surprised when Miranda caught up with her.

"I saw Paxton give you the papers," Miranda said in a low voice. "When do we leave?"

Beatrice still didn't trust her cousin, but they needed Miranda to show them the way to Dally Rumpe's cave.

"In the morning," Beatrice told her. "We leave for the gnome village before dawn."

The desert cookout was that night, and Beatrice was determined to go. She knew that Ira would see this as further proof that Beatrice was lazy and irresponsible, but she refused to feel guilty. In the morning—if all went well— they would be going inside Blood Mountain, and this might be their last evening of fun. She tried not to think that this could be their last evening *period*.

Beatrice and her friends arrived at the stables a little before midnight. Beatrice had tied a bright bandana around Cayenne's neck, and the cat was strutting around looking very pleased with herself. Seamus was there, as well as most of the campers, including Kasper. Uri and Longfellow were leading horses out of the stalls. The gnome handed Plum's reins to Beatrice.

"Hello there, girl," Beatrice said, happy to see the purple horse again.

Kasper was looking anxiously at the chestnut mare that he was supposed to ride. "I don't know if this is such a good idea," the boy muttered.

"You'll do fine," Uri assured him. "Honeybun is as sweet as her name."

Kasper swung himself into the saddle, but he looked even more nervous as he peered down at the ground.

"Since we don't have that far to go, we won't be flying tonight," Uri said from atop a beautiful black mare. "All right, let's get started."

Cayenne settled herself in front of Beatrice, and Beatrice tapped Plum's sides gently with her heels.

As they started out across the desert, Beatrice tried not to look at the red sun over Blood Mountain. Its garish glow triggered horrible images in her mind, making her think of lumbering giants and piles of bones picked clean by birds of prey. Then they turned east and the fiery mountain was to their backs. The desert seemed to stretch out endlessly before them, lit only by stars and a glorious silver moon.

They rode for about half an hour through the cool night air, and Beatrice enjoyed every minute of it. Finally, Uri led them down a slope and into a shallow bowl surrounded by giant cacti.

Uri stopped his horse and said, "Well, here we are."

In the bright moonlight, Beatrice could see the charred remains of a campfire and a large pile of new wood stacked off to the side.

When they had dismounted from their horses, Uri raised his hands into the air and clapped twice. Suddenly the cacti that encircled the bowl lit up like Christmas trees, glowing with thousands of twinkling white lights.

Everyone ooohed and ahhhed in delight until a grinning Uri told them to make themselves useful. Soon the campers were carrying wood to build a fire, while Beatrice and her friends helped Seamus set the food out on a flat-topped boulder. Before long, Uri was cooking their meal over a blazing fire.

Seamus served up bowls of horned-toad chilli, while Beatrice and Teddy filled the campers' plates with devil dogs and brimstone baked beans. Cyrus was thrilled. There was nothing he liked better than a hot dog smothered in mustard.

When they had finished off the last of the food, they sat around the fire singing songs. Beatrice and her friends didn't know the words so they hummed along while the others sang. The campers' favorite seemed to be a song called "Boo!" because they kept singing it over and over with earsplitting enthusiasm.

Out in the desert, where the moon shines bright,
Rides a coven of witches 'most every night.
There's tall ones and short ones, and skinny ones, too,
And once in a while, a ghost shouting, "Boo!"
Some riding horses and some riding brooms,
They fly across the desert singing cowboy tunes.

And likely as not, you'll see them there, too,
This coven of witches and a ghost shouting, "Boo!"

It was nearly three in the morning when they started back to the ranch. Beatrice was having a hard time keeping her eyes open.

Riding beside her, Teddy yawned noisily. "We have to meet the gnomes in a couple of hours," she said in a groggy voice. "If I fall asleep in the mines, don't you dare go off and leave me."

Beatrice groaned. She hadn't given any thought to how tired they would be after getting back so late. And they needed to be alert when they went into the tunnels—not to mention, Dally Rumpe's cave. Who knew what they would have to deal with there?

"I didn't plan this very well," Beatrice admitted. "But we can't back out now. The gnomes are expecting us, and they've probably gone to a lot of trouble with our disguises."

She turned around in her saddle to see how Ollie and Cyrus were doing. Ollie seemed fine, but Cyrus was slumped across his horse's neck fast asleep.

We're going to need a lot of luck, Beatrice thought.

14

The Sorcerer's Cave

*B*eatrice slept for about an hour and then got up to take a shower. It didn't help much. She was still yawning, and her head felt like it was stuffed with wet cotton when she left a groggy Teddy and started down the stairs with Cayenne in her arms. Beatrice found Joy in the kitchen, watching as a big lump of biscuit dough rolled itself out for cutting.

Joy looked up and blew a strand of hair out of her face. "So you're leaving now?" She was obviously trying to sound cheerful, but her furrowed brow gave her away. "If you and your friends can wait a few minutes, I'll scramble you some serpent's eggs."

"Thanks, but we're still full from the cookout," Beatrice said.

"Well, take these, anyway," Joy said, handing Beatrice a bag of warm mosquito muffins. "And don't worry about Cayenne. She can hang out in the kitchen with me and be my official taster."

Hearing that, Cayenne leaped from Beatrice's arms to a tall stool and sat waiting expectantly.

Beatrice and Joy smiled at the cat.

"Do you have your papers?" Joy asked, looking worried again.

Beatrice patted the pocket of her jeans. "Right here."

"I know I talked Paxton into helping you," Joy said, "but maybe that wasn't such a smart idea. You can still change your mind."

"It's going to be okay," Beatrice assured her, feigning more confidence than she felt. "We've come out all right three times now."

"But you've never faced Blood Mountain," Joy said bluntly. "Be very careful, Beatrice. And if you get inside the mountain and see that it's too risky to try to make it to the top, come back down with the gnomes. Promise me."

"I promise to be careful," Beatrice said. "And thanks for taking care of my girl."

Beatrice kissed the top of Cayenne's head and left quickly, before her better judgment could kick in.

Teddy, Ollie, Cyrus, and Miranda were waiting for her in the lobby. With the exception of Miranda, they all looked seriously sleep deprived. Beatrice passed out the muffins and they chewed without much appetite as they crossed the desert toward Winged-Horse Mountain. Except for the crimson glow of Blood Mountain, it was still dark outside. A thin line of gold was just beginning to show along the horizon.

When they reached the path that led into the gnome village, Cyrus chanted the shrinking spell, making them all two feet tall. Miranda sat down heavily on the ground and held her head until it quit spinning. The others had been feeling light-headed, anyway, and didn't notice much difference.

The miners were waiting for them inside O. Henry's cottage.

"You need to hurry," Marietta said to Beatrice, and began to hand out clothing and beards. "The men have to leave in a few minutes. You can dress in the bedrooms," she added, pointing to two doorways.

Beatrice, Teddy, and Miranda found themselves in a tiny chamber that was dominated by a bed stacked high with down comforters and fluffy pillows. The only other piece of furniture in the room was a wardrobe that looked handmade, with delicate carvings of gnomes riding jackrabbits and peeking out from behind rocks and cacti.

Beatrice pulled on the gray shirt and trousers. When she sat on the bed to put on her socks and boots, she sank up to her shoulders in plushy comforters.

"This isn't easy," she muttered, struggling to get up again.

Beatrice pulled her hair back with a rubber band, and then held the red beard to her face, looping curved arms like those on eyeglasses over her ears to hold it in place.

"Wow," Teddy murmured. "You look like a real gnome! That beard even matches your eyebrows."

Ollie and Cyrus, already dressed and bearded, were waiting for them in the main room. Marietta and O. Henry eyed the witches critically.

"I think you'll pass inspection," Marietta said finally.

"They're a little thin," O. Henry remarked. "What about stuffing their shirts with pillows?"

"Not a good idea," Marietta answered promptly. "Pillows would slide around and end up poking out in odd places. They aren't much skinnier than some of the younger men."

O. Henry gave them each a hard hat with a light affixed to the top, and Chaucer handed out picks and small blue pails.

"We use these picks to cut through the rock," Chaucer told them, demonstrating by raising the wooden handle over his shoulder and lowering its pointed metal head toward the floor. "When we find a ruby, we dig it out carefully and drop it into the pail."

That doesn't sound too hard, Beatrice thought. Then she went to lift her pick and its weight nearly jerked her arms out of their sockets.

Chaucer grinned. "You'd better not do that in front of the Ghumbabas," he said. "A mining pick is as light as a moonbeam to a gnome."

"We carry our papers in our shirt pocket," O. Henry told them, "so they're easy to get out when we reach the entrance to the tunnels."

Beatrice and her companions were hurriedly stuffing papers into their pockets and trying to lift the heavy picks as the real miners began to stream out the door.

The gnomes fell into line single file as they walked toward Blood Mountain, arranging themselves so that the witches were sandwiched approximately in the middle. As they approached the row of mining carts at the base of the mountain, the temperature started to rise. Beatrice began to sweat and itch under the fluffy beard. It felt like she had a chinchilla clinging to her face.

Paxton was standing near the tracks, directing gnomes into the carts. He was frowning as his eyes swept over the gathered miners, lingering for an instant on Beatrice and Teddy, then moving away deliberately.

Beatrice and the other witches crowded into a cart with Chaucer. They tried to look as nonchalant as the gnome, but when the cart suddenly lurched and started speeding up the mountain, they had to grab hold of its sides to keep from tumbling out.

It was a bumpy and clattery ride. Beatrice clamped her teeth together to keep them from chattering as the cart bounced up the tracks. She was afraid to look down—the mountain was a lot higher than it had seemed from the ground—so she tilted her head back and looked skyward. The brilliant crimson sun was blinding, and the air was so hot it took her breath away. Above the tallest peaks, at least a dozen enormous birds of prey were circling lazily, waiting. At the sight of the birds, Beatrice's stomach flip-flopped and she dropped her eyes hastily.

The cart finally leveled off and came to a stop on a wide stone ledge. In front of them was the dark yawning mouth of the tunnel. And standing beside the entrance to the mines was the most horrible creature Beatrice had ever seen.

It was at least twenty feet tall, its green-gray body reminding Beatrice of a disgusting lump of moldy bread. Long bulging arms and thick legs protruded from a tunic that was little more than greasy rags.

As Beatrice and her companions stared fearfully at the Ghumbaba, it stared back at them through tiny pinpoint eyes, its bloated lips hanging open stupidly and glistening with saliva. Even more repulsive were the pulsing veins that roped across its bald head and the clusters of hairy warts on its broad flat nose and doughy chin.

Leaning toward them, the giant grunted, a rasping phlegmy sound that made Beatrice nearly gag.

"He wants to see your papers," Chaucer whispered out of the side of his mouth.

Beatrice dug into her pocket and produced the papers, her hand trembling as she held them out to the giant. His mouth fell open even wider as he studied the document, revealing nubs of rotted teeth. Then he handed the papers back to Beatrice and turned his small dull eyes on Chaucer.

The gnome shoved Beatrice forward and she stumbled into the cool darkness of the mine. Heart pounding, she waited for the others to file silently into the tunnel.

"You did fine," Chaucer assured them softly when they were all assembled. "Turn on your lights and come with me."

They followed him down a long, wide tunnel that led toward the center of the mountain, the beams of light on their hats bouncing off the stone walls as they walked. When they came to a smaller tunnel branching off from the main one, Chaucer stopped. Most of the gnomes were already at work there, splitting piles of rocks with their picks.

"Continue on to the end of the tunnel," Chaucer said to Beatrice. "The passageway that leads up to the top of the mountain will be on your right. If it hasn't been finished and you need to go back down with us, be sure you're here by six o'clock. We won't be able to wait for you."

"Thanks for your help," Beatrice said, but Chaucer had already turned his back and was lifting his pick over his head.

Beatrice and her companions dropped their own picks and pails and started walking.

"All right, Miranda," Teddy said, "where's Dally Rumpe's cave?"

"It should be nearby," Miranda answered, peering closely at the left-hand wall as they continued through the tunnel.

"*Should* be?" Teddy echoed. "I thought you knew exactly where to find it."

"I'm trying to locate the entrance," Miranda snapped, and then came to an abrupt halt. "There!" she said triumphantly, pointing to a narrow crevice in the stone. "This is how you get to the cave—it's just as Dally Rumpe described it."

The opening was less than two feet high. Ollie had to stoop to direct the light on his hat inside. "It's another tunnel," he said. "And a twisty one, at that. I can only see a few feet ahead."

Bending down beside him, Miranda slipped through the crevice and disappeared.

"You can stand up once you're inside," came Miranda's muffled voice.

No one else had made a move to follow her. Now Teddy whispered to Beatrice, "Do we really want to do this? She could be leading us into a trap."

"I know," Beatrice whispered back. "But if Dally Rumpe's spellbook is in there, I want to see it."

"I wonder how Dally Rumpe even found this," Ollie muttered. "Unless he can shrink himself, he must have had to crawl in on his belly."

"Hey!" Miranda shouted, the word echoing through the tunnel. "Are you guys coming—or are you going to stand there whispering all day?"

"We're coming," Beatrice said, and stooping down, slipped through the crevice.

The passageway was low and narrow, but roomy enough for them to walk upright without touching the ceiling or the sides.

"The cave shouldn't be too far from here," Miranda said.

"Then let's get going," Teddy replied, and fell into step behind Miranda.

The tunnel twisted and turned every few feet; they had to be careful not to go so fast that they'd end up walking into a rock wall. Unlike the outside of Blood Mountain, the interior was cool and comfortable, but Beatrice's face still itched. She jerked off the scratchy beard and tucked it into the waistband of her trousers.

They followed the winding passageway for what seemed like a very long time, until finally, the tunnel opened up into a cavern about the size of a baseball diamond, its vaulted ceiling at least thirty feet high. A shaft of light streamed down through a hole in the ceiling, giving the cavern a rosy glow.

"This is it," Miranda said softly. "Dally Rumpe's cave."

They stood close together at the edge of the cavern, their eyes darting anxiously into every shadowy corner. Beatrice thought she heard the trickle of water, and looking in the direction of the sound, saw a stream running through the center of the cave. Had they been their normal size, they could have waded through it, but it was at least as deep as their two-foot height and three times as wide.

On the other side of the stream was a pallet of straw covered with a ragged blanket. A large cauldron squatted over a pile of charred wood and dead ash.

"Someone's had a fire," Ollie observed, "and fairly recently. I can still smell the smoke."

Beatrice tensed, glancing around again to see if anyone was lurking in the shadows. Then her eyes fell on what appeared to be a natural shelf carved into the wall above the makeshift bed. There was a rusty lantern on the shelf, and beside it, a thick book, its red leather binding brittle and faded.

"The spellbook," Beatrice said softly.

Miranda let out a sharp excited cry and started toward the book. She halted, frowning, at the edge of the stream.

"Make me big again," she demanded, looking over her shoulder at Cyrus.

"Make us *all* big," Teddy said, cutting her eyes at Miranda.

They held hands while Cyrus repeated the spell. As soon as they were normal size again, Miranda started splashing through the stream, but Beatrice was faster. She sprinted ahead of Miranda, through the water and across the pile of straw—and grabbed the book first!

Beatrice had just enough time to see *Book of Spells* imprinted in tarnished gold across the cover before Miranda's hand darted out to take it. Beatrice jerked the book out of her reach. On the other side of the stream, Teddy, Ollie, and Cyrus were grinning, but Miranda was fit to be tied.

"I'm the one who brought you here," Miranda sputtered. "You wouldn't have even *known* about the cave if not for me. *I* should be allowed to look at the spellbook first."

"Honestly, Miranda," Teddy said. "Will you please stop whining?"

Beatrice cradled the spellbook protectively against her chest, thinking that they should leave the cave before they examined it—just in case Dally Rumpe was nearby. But then she noticed movement out of the corner of her eye.

She spun around, her heart thumping against her ribs, and saw them. Spiders! There were hundreds of them—black and hairy and as big as a man's fist—skittering out of crevices in the wall above the bed, moving swiftly down the rough stone, and heading en masse for Beatrice.

They must be the protectors of the spellbook, Beatrice thought wildly and made a dash for the stream. But not fast enough. She felt something tickle her leg and glanced down to see at least twenty spiders climbing up her trousers.

Teddy and Cyrus were screaming something unintelligible, and Ollie was running through the water toward Beatrice shouting, "They're lethal! Dr. Meadowmouse said—one bite—"

One bite and I'm dead, Beatrice thought hysterically, and began to kick her legs furiously and beat at the spiders with the spellbook. But the spiders held on, creeping higher and higher. Up her calves, past her knees—

Now it was Beatrice's turn to scream.

15

Book of Spells

Spiders were skittering up Beatrice's thighs. In total panic, she started to run. But the next thing she knew, someone had thrown their full weight against her and she crashed to the hard stone floor.

Twisting around, she saw Miranda's face swimming above her own. Beatrice was stunned. Why had Miranda tackled her? Did she mean to hold Beatrice down until the spiders finished her off?

Beatrice stared in bewilderment at Miranda, whose expression was decidedly grim, and saw that her cousin was holding some kind of cloth. The blanket from Dally Rumpe's bed! Miranda shook out the blanket and it billowed in the air—before floating down to cover Beatrice from head to foot. The coarse fabric settled over her eyes and nose, shutting out the dim light. The odors of unwashed flesh and damp stinking wool filled Beatrice's nostrils. She started to scream, but only succeeded in sucking the filthy blanket into her mouth. It was smothering her!

Beatrice began to flail against the weight of Miranda's body, but Miranda had wrapped the blanket tightly around Beatrice, immobilizing her arms and legs. With her face covered, Beatrice couldn't see anything, but she felt Miranda hitting her. *Hard!*

Teddy, Ollie, and Cyrus were shouting something, obviously agitated, but Beatrice couldn't make out the words. Dazed and frightened, she didn't understand what was going on. Why weren't her friends helping her? Why didn't they pull Miranda off?

Beatrice rolled and twisted, gasping for air through the nasty blanket. It was a nightmare! She was going to die. Miranda was going to kill her.

And then, suddenly, the blanket was yanked off.

Beatrice looked up at the faces staring down at her. All three of her friends, pale with fear and worry—and Miranda. While gulping down air, Beatrice focused on her cousin's face, and was startled to see that Miranda looked just as scared as the others!

"What—?" Beatrice croaked, trying to sit up. "What were you doing to me?" she yelled at Miranda.

"The spiders," Ollie began, and Beatrice leaped to her feet. She had forgotten all about the spiders! But when she looked down at her legs, she saw that they were gone.

"Miranda wrapped the blanket about you," Cyrus said, his blue eyes huge in his small face, "and crushed the spiders."

"Before they could reach bare skin," Ollie added, and pointed to the blanket. "See?"

Within its tattered and dirty folds, Beatrice could see the crumpled bodies of a lot of spiders.

"And the others went back into their holes," Cyrus said.

Beatrice's eyes darted to the wall around the shelf. No sign of a spider anywhere.

"I guess they saw what was happening to their friends," Ollie said, still deathly pale but trying to smile, "and decided to split."

Beatrice turned to look at Miranda, who had removed the gnome beard and was using it to calmly blot the sweat off her face.

"Those spiders are deadly," Beatrice said slowly. "If only one had bitten me—"

"Now, don't go getting syrupy on me," Miranda cut in, frowning. "If you had died, the Witches Executive Committee would have jerked the rest of us out of here so fast, we wouldn't have had a chance to break the spell. Besides," she added coolly, "with my checkered past, they'd have probably blamed your untimely demise on *me*."

A hint of a smile tugged at Beatrice's lips. "It couldn't have been that you wanted to help me," she said, "that deep down, you really aren't such a bad witch after all."

"Not a chance," Miranda snapped, and stood up abruptly. "I don't know about you, but I don't intend to wait around for those spiders to come back. I'm getting out of here."

"Good idea," Ollie said, and held out a hand to help Beatrice to her feet.

Teddy had been strangely quiet, watching Miranda through narrowed eyes. Now she said gruffly, "That was quick thinking, Miranda. I'm not sure I would have thought of throwing the blanket over Beatrice."

Miranda just scowled at her.

"I'll need to shrink us again if we don't want to crawl out on our bellies," Cyrus said. And he did.

"Have you got the spellbook?" Miranda asked Beatrice as they entered the passageway to the main tunnel.

"Right here," Beatrice said, holding up the book, which had also shrunk.

When they reached the main tunnel, they started again toward the center of the mountain. A half hour later, the tunnel came to an end. But another small passageway, hardly bigger than a rabbit's hole, branched off to the right.

"This must be the tunnel that leads to the top of the mountain," Ollie said, peering inside.

"Well, what are you waiting for?" Miranda demanded, and brushing past him, ducked into the opening.

The others scurried after her.

The passageway was just large enough for them to walk upright; but the tunnel rose steeply, making it a difficult climb. The space was so tight, their shoulders kept brushing against the rocky sides.

"This is creepy," Cyrus said a while later, his voice sounding high-pitched and anxious. "I think I'm getting claustrophobia."

"It's better than facing the Ghumbabas, isn't it?" Beatrice asked.

But then she stumbled into Miranda and realized that her cousin had come to a stop.

"This is as far as it goes," Miranda said.

And sure enough, just ahead, Beatrice saw that the passageway ended with a rock wall.

"I can't believe it," Teddy muttered.

Beatrice had never been more disappointed. How were they ever going to get to the top of the mountain now?

"We'd better start back," Ollie said wearily.

They turned around slowly in the tight space and began to trudge down the passageway.

"Well, at least we got the spellbook," Beatrice said, trying to find something to cheer them up.

"Let's hope there's a spell to make giants and birds of prey disappear," Teddy grumbled.

When they reached the tunnel where the gnomes were working, Chaucer lowered his pick and watched their approach. "No way to the top?" he asked.

"Afraid not," Ollie answered glumly.

"We might as well help you till it's time to leave," Beatrice said.

She found one of the picks they had discarded and dragged it over to a pile of rocks. Chaucer smiled slightly. Shaking his head, he went back to work.

As soon as they got back to the ranch, Beatrice took a shower and washed the dust and grime from her hair. She was coming out to tell Teddy that the bathroom was all hers when she nearly ran into Miranda, who was skulking outside the door.

"Where's the spellbook?" Miranda demanded.

Teddy, Ollie, and Cyrus were perched on the edge of Teddy's bed, still filthy and disheveled from their day in the mines.

"We're all anxious to look at it," Teddy admitted.

Beatrice raised her eyebrows. Teddy's vanity usually ensured that she attend to her appearance before anything else.

"It's right here," Beatrice said, and pulled the book out from the towel she was holding.

"You took it into the bathroom with you?" Miranda asked incredulously.

"Can't be too careful," Beatrice muttered, noticing that someone had ransacked her backpack and left socks and underwear spilling out on the bed. She gave her cousin a withering look.

"Okay, let's see it," Miranda said.

Beatrice sat down on Teddy's bed and everyone leaned closer as she opened the book. The name *Dalbert Bailiwick* was scrawled inside the cover. The first page was the Table of Contents, where spells were listed under three headings.

"'*Part 1: To Torment an Enemy*,'" Beatrice read aloud. "'*Part 2: To Maim or Kill an Enemy. Part 3: To Take Over the World*.'"

"Sounds pretty heavy," Cyrus said uneasily. "I guess evil wizards aren't interested in love spells."

On the next page were just two sentences. Beatrice read, "'*Only those sorcerers with great and terrible powers should attempt to cast these spells. All others are doomed to fail!*'"

"Well, that's simple and to the point," Ollie said dryly. "Turn the page and let's see what damage great and terrible sorcerers can do."

Beatrice flipped to the first spell and they all read it to themselves.

"Hey—that's not too awful," Cyrus said. "I wouldn't mind being able to work this one on some of the kids at school."

Miranda gave him a sour look. "There's no way you'd be able to cast any of these spells—even one this simple."

"Is that so?" Cyrus glared at her. "Come on, everybody, hold hands," he said fiercely. "No, not you, Teddy. I'm going to cast the spell on you."

Teddy was taken aback. "Not that I think for a minute that you'll be able to do it," she said bluntly, "but I don't remember volunteering to be your guinea pig."

Ollie was smiling. "Come on, Teddy, be a sport."

Teddy cut her eyes at Cyrus. "All right," she muttered, "give it all you've got. But if it does work, you won't have to worry about the giants—I'll shove you off a cliff myself."

Cyrus just grinned.

"Here goes," he said, and began to chant:

> *Those inside the circle are safe from harm,*
> *Only those outside will feel this charm.*
> *Give Teddy warts all over, I do decree,*
> *And what a hideous sight she'll be!*

No one was too surprised when nothing happened, but Teddy still looked relieved when she peered into the mirror and saw that no warts had popped up.

"It's my turn," Teddy said, grabbing the book.

She tried to work the same spell on Cyrus, and again, nothing happened. Cyrus started to laugh and collapsed on the bed. Teddy was disgruntled by her failure, to say the least.

Ollie had been reading the next spell. "Let me try one," he said.

From the air, from the sky,
Wherever stinkbugs lurk,
Come fill this room, as I bid,
And do my evil work.

Miranda was peering around with a smug smile. "Well, I don't see any stinkbugs," she said sarcastically. "Or maybe they're shy. Could they be hiding, do you think?"

"Why don't you try it?" Teddy snapped.

"All right, I will," Miranda replied.

She chanted the stinkbug spell, but was no more successful than Ollie. Teddy couldn't have looked more pleased.

"Let's stop goofing around," Beatrice said impatiently. "We should read the part about taking over the world and see if we can find a spell Dally Rumpe might have used to take Bailiwick from Bromwich."

"Yeah," Ollie said as he peered over Miranda's shoulder at the book. "It gives a way to reverse each spell. Maybe we won't even have to climb Blood Mountain."

"Not so fast," Miranda said sharply, apparently still stinging from her unsuccessful attempt at conjuring up stinkbugs. "Beatrice, *you* haven't tried to cast a spell yet."

"What's the point?" Beatrice demanded. "If none of you could get one to work, I won't be able to."

"*Try,*" Miranda said.

"Oh, all right."

Beatrice jerked the book away from Miranda and started to mutter a halfhearted stinkbug spell. She had just said the last word, and was looking at her cousin as if to say, *Are you satisfied now?* when she noticed hundreds of tiny black dots moving in front of her eyes. And she smelled a horrible odor.

"Oh, my gosh," Teddy said under her breath, and began to smack at the minuscule bugs lighting on her face.

"Beatrice," Ollie said, staring at her in awe, "you did it."

Cyrus was shaking his head frantically. "Some just flew into my ear!" he shouted.

Thousands of bugs were swarming, bringing with them a smell that was a cross between rotten eggs and an open sewer. Beatrice couldn't believe it. She was so stunned she barely noticed the bugs landing on the tips of her eyelashes.

"Do something!" Miranda shouted, slapping at stinkbugs that were trying to crawl up her nostrils.

Beatrice's eyes dropped to the spellbook. The room was now so thick with bugs, she could barely see the words. She held the book closer and chanted haltingly:

Undo this charm so pests will flee,
As my word, so mote it be.

The stinkbugs disappeared.

Beatrice looked around at the faces of her friends, who were all clearly shocked, and then at Miranda. Her cousin appeared to be the most shocked of all—not to mention, the most jealous.

"Why can you cast one of Dally Rumpe's spells, and I can't?" Miranda burst out. "I'm a lot more terrible than you are!"

"I'll be happy to switch places with you," Beatrice said, her voice shaking. In fact, her whole body was beginning to tremble. She turned terrified eyes to Ollie. "I don't *want* to be able to cast this kind of spell."

"Just because you can, doesn't mean you're evil," Ollie said quickly.

"Of course not," Teddy agreed. "This was just a fluke."

Miranda was staring hard at Beatrice. "Try another one."

"Not likely," Beatrice snapped.

"Then you'll never know, will you?" Miranda asked. "*Was* it just a fluke—or do you have evil powers?"

Beatrice cringed at the words.

"Maybe you *should* try another spell," Ollie said quietly. He turned to the next page in the book. "I'll bet you anything it won't work. Then you'll see that there's nothing to worry about, right?"

"I guess so," Beatrice muttered.

She looked down at the book, and reluctantly began to chant:

> *Once good friends, now we will see,*
> *Teddy and Cyrus as enemies.*
> *Thus, I bid, so mote it be.*

For a moment, no one said anything. Beatrice was just about to breathe a sigh of relief when Teddy suddenly glared at Cyrus and said, "What are you doing in my room? You aren't welcome here!"

Beatrice thought this might be Teddy's warped idea of a joke until she saw the ugly expression on Cyrus's face.

"Make me leave," he snarled. "Come on, I dare you!"

Everyone was staring at Teddy and Cyrus in astonishment when Teddy leaped up, her fists positioned in front of her like a boxer's.

"I'll make you leave all right," Teddy said through clenched teeth. "Face me like a man! Unless you're too scared."

Cyrus sprang from the bed, his face registering fury and loathing.

"Hold on!" Ollie exclaimed, and jumped between the two.

Teddy and Cyrus were trying to get around Ollie, throwing jabs and punches as they shouted insults at each other. Ollie was getting the worst part of it, especially when Cyrus's fist landed solidly in his belly.

Ollie groaned and bent over, giving Teddy the opportunity to hit Cyrus squarely on the nose.

Beatrice had been watching numbly, too astonished to move. But when Ollie shouted for her to reverse the spell, while trying to hold Teddy and Cyrus off with outstretched arms, Beatrice snapped out of her daze. She found the reversal spell and began to mutter hastily:

> Undo this charm so hate will flee,
> As my word, so mote it be.

Everyone stood utterly still, Teddy and Cyrus's fists still raised in the air near Ollie's head. Beatrice thought they looked like statues, though very peculiar ones—

especially Ollie, whose expression seemed frozen in permanent pain.

Teddy and Cyrus slowly lowered their fists and stepped back, looking perplexed and then ashamed.

"Gosh," Cyrus squeaked, "I'm sorry, Teddy. I don't know what came over me."

"Yeah," Teddy said hurriedly, "I'm—uh—sorry I punched you in the nose."

But Miranda hadn't taken her eyes off Beatrice.

"You did it," Miranda said, staring at Beatrice with an expression of wonder.

Beatrice had a wild look, like she might start screaming—or slugging someone herself. Ollie came over and put an arm around her shoulders.

"I don't understand how you were able to cast the spells," he said gently, "but I know it's not because you're evil."

Teddy and Cyrus had now returned to normal and were quick to back Ollie up.

"You're anything *but* evil," Cyrus said emphatically.

"Yeah, Beatrice, you're a lot nicer than I am," Teddy declared, and then with a sigh, added quietly, "and a lot more powerful, too, it seems."

Beatrice jerked her head around to look at Teddy. "I'm *not* powerful, and I don't want to *be* powerful," she cried. "Not *that* way. Not like *him!*"

"You aren't like him," Ollie assured her.

"But she can work his spells," Miranda pointed out, still looking awestruck. "It was easy for you, Beatrice. I'll bet you could cast any spell in this book."

Beatrice turned pale as fear shot through her. She thought she was going to be sick.

"It's written in the book," Beatrice said weakly, "that only sorcerers with great and *terrible* powers are able to work these spells. So that must mean that I *am* evil. Don't forget, I have Dally Rumpe's blood running through my veins," she finished miserably.

"So do I," Miranda shot back, scowling. "But as usual, Beatrice, you've had all the luck."

Beatrice just stared at her cousin as if she couldn't believe what Miranda had said.

Meanwhile, Ollie had been looking through the spell-book.

"I don't see anything that Dally Rumpe could have used whole to cast his spell on Bailiwick," Ollie said, still flipping pages. "He might have combined spells—or created a new one."

"So we won't find a way in the book to reverse it," Teddy said.

"Who cares?" Miranda burst out, her gray eyes glittering like sunlight on ice. "We have something better!"

Miranda looked slyly at Beatrice. "You can use the spells in this book against Dally Rumpe. Okay," she added hastily, seeing the panic in Beatrice's face, "I know you couldn't bring yourself to kill him—but what about maiming him? Just a little. Just enough to keep him out of our hair until we've found Bromwich's daughter—what's her name again?—and you've repeated the counterspell."

"I'm not going to use his evil spells," Beatrice replied stiffly.

"Wait a minute—let's think about this," Teddy said, her eyebrows drawn together in concentration. "I don't see anything wrong with using evil spells to *fight* evil.

Beatrice, you could cast spells on the giants and the birds of prey, too."

"No, Teddy," Beatrice said.

"All right," Teddy muttered in exasperation. "Then what do you propose we do?"

"We'll find another way," Ollie said.

"I *knew* it," Miranda grumbled. "You people are too *soft* to go after Dally Rumpe. Now do you see why *I* should have been the one to break the Bailiwick spell?"

16

The Hunter's Path

Since they had missed lunch and dinner, and every-one was ravenous—even Beatrice, despite being worried sick about her newly discovered powers—Ollie and Cyrus left to raid the kitchen. Miranda stomped out after them, muttering under her breath that life was totally unfair.

Teddy watched Beatrice pace back and forth across the floor. Finally, Beatrice came to a halt and looked at Teddy.

"If I used the spells in this book," Beatrice burst out, "I wouldn't be any better than Dally Rumpe! I can't do it, Teddy."

"I know," Teddy said, but there was regret in her voice. "I guess I let my competitive nature get out of hand. See, Beatrice? You really are a lot nicer than I am."

"No, I'm not," Beatrice said darkly. "When Miranda said I should use the spells against Dally Rumpe, I was tempted. *Horrified*, but still—to have a chance to beat him just thrown into our laps. How could I *not* consider it?"

"Well, you've made the right choice," Teddy said with slightly more conviction. "We'll have to come up with another way to get past the giants and the birds of prey."

"I just thought of something," Beatrice said. She sat down heavily on the edge of her bed. "Winifred Stoop predicted this!"

"What do you mean?"

"Winifred's dream. She said I'd have to choose between good and evil—and that it wouldn't be as clearly defined as I imagined."

Teddy had a peculiar look on her face. "Kind of creepy, isn't it?"

"That's one word for it," Beatrice muttered.

She was feeling overwhelmed. The thought of using Dally Rumpe's spells repulsed her, but how else were they going to make it up that mountain? What was she supposed to do? Put her friends in mortal danger when there was a safer way? But how safe was it to use dark magic? How could she even think about doing it? Beatrice stared numbly out the window at the glowing crimson peaks of Blood Mountain. She wasn't sure that she even knew who she was anymore.

The dining room was buzzing when Beatrice and her friends went down to breakfast the next morning. Everyone seemed to be talking at once, and there was an undercurrent of excitement in their voices.

As Beatrice sat down between Cayenne and Ollie, she noticed that most heads were turned toward a table in a corner, where a young guy was sitting with two gray-haired men. Beatrice couldn't see much more than the tops of their heads over their menus, but it was hard to miss the young man's spiked hair, which had been dyed a brilliant shade of green.

"Who are those men?" Beatrice asked when Fairlamb came to take their orders.

"You don't know?" Fairlamb exclaimed, her blue eyes round with astonishment. "Why that's Blesma Soul, the rock star." She gave Beatrice a look that implied she should get out more. "Don't you just love his hair? Last time he was here, it was bright pink."

"Who are the guys with him?" Ollie asked.

Fairlamb shrugged, as if the older men were of no consequence whatsoever. "His manager—and his publicist, I think. Blesma's been giving concerts all over the Sphere, and he's come here to rest for a couple of days. We're supposed to tell the guests not to bother him for autographs and pictures," she added, giving them all a severe look.

"Not to worry," Beatrice said lightly, and bent her head to study the menu.

Still hungry after their day without food, they ordered a little of everything, and were just digging in when Ollie happened to glance toward the door.

"Oh, no," he muttered. "Don't look now, but your biggest fan has returned."

Beatrice's head jerked up and her heart sank when she saw Hyacinth Broomshead framed in the doorway.

"Hold on to your napkin," Cyrus said with a frown.

"What's *she* doing back here?" Teddy demanded.

Beatrice's eyes drifted from Hyacinth to Blesma Soul. "It's only a guess," she said dryly, "but maybe she wants to sell some green hair on the Witch World Web."

"I hope that's all it is," Ollie said thoughtfully.

Just then, Ira Skelly came barreling into the room, nearly bumping into Hyacinth. The red-haired witch scowled at him before making her way to Joy and Seamus's table.

"Another delightful surprise," Beatrice said grimly, and slumped lower in her chair.

But Ira had seen them and was already heading their way.

Beatrice sighed and put down her fork.

Not bothering to greet them, Ira's small dark eyes impaled Beatrice. "I've spoken with Dr. Featherstone," he said brusquely.

"And?" Teddy prompted.

"She said that she has no authority over mortal studies. Whether Beatrice takes advantage of my superior tutoring is entirely voluntary."

Beatrice perked up. "Really?"

"I told you Dr. F didn't give a hoot about your exam," Teddy said to Beatrice.

"I must say," Ollie remarked, regarding the tutor closely, "that you don't seem especially bothered about your vacation being cut short."

"This trip was hardly a vacation," Ira said haughtily. "I came here to gather data for my research."

"Oh. And I thought you came to tutor Beatrice," Teddy said pleasantly.

"Of course—that, too," Ira said with a dismissive wave of his hand. "But Joy has kindly allowed me several interviews. As a witch living under prolonged stress, you understand. A few more discussions with her, and I should have all the information I need."

"Right," Cyrus said with a devilish grin. "But shouldn't you be talking to more than one witch?"

"Not necessary," Ira snapped.

"I imagine you'll be leaving soon," Beatrice said, unable to conceal her hope that this was true.

"Actually," Ira said, looking pleased, "Dr. Featherstone has been kind enough to suggest that I take a few days off, so I plan to stay here and finish my work."

It occurred to Beatrice that Dr. Featherstone was probably happy to have him out of her hair.

"But she said I was to inform you," Ira continued, his expression becoming stern, "that I'll be available should you decide to take your studies seriously."

Beatrice doubted that Dr. Featherstone had phrased it just that way, but she smiled politely at Ira. "Thank you," she said. "I'll certainly keep that in mind."

After Ira had left for Joy's table, Ollie said, "We'd better start thinking about how we're going to climb Blood Mountain."

Beatrice couldn't help feeling guilty. Here she was refusing to use the spellbook, and she didn't have a single alternative in mind.

"Trying it at night won't help," Teddy said, sprinkling some sugar-coated ants on her cereal, "with that red sun lighting up everything like a search beacon."

Beatrice found that she was no longer hungry. "I think I'll go for a walk," she said.

"Why don't we all go?" Ollie said. "Maybe some fresh air will clear our minds."

As they left the dining room, Beatrice looked around and noticed that Miranda was nowhere to be seen, but Hyacinth Broomshead's eyes were following them to the door. Wasn't that witch ever going to give up?

A few minutes later, Beatrice and her friends were approaching the stables. Cayenne ran ahead and leaped to the top rail of the corral fence to peer in at the horses. Beatrice was starting after the cat when she looked up and saw Balto flying over Blood Mountain.

"I was wondering what had happened to the old guy," Ollie said, stopping to watch the horse's graceful glide over the summit. "He hasn't started a fire in ages, has he? I don't care what you say, Beatrice, I think you've taught him some manners."

"Too bad he won't let anyone near him," Teddy said. "He could carry us to the top of the mountain in ten seconds flat."

But Beatrice was no longer listening. She had noticed someone standing just inside the stable door, watching them. It couldn't be Longfellow. Too tall. Uri, maybe. But why was he lurking around so secretively? Beatrice still didn't trust Uri—although her confidence in Miranda had risen a notch since the girl had saved her from the spiders, and Miranda had trusted Uri enough to reveal her true identity to him. Beatrice decided it was time to talk to Uri, and started toward the stables. But then she realized that it wasn't Uri standing there at all. It was Orion.

Beatrice couldn't see the hunter's eyes under his hood, but it was obvious that his attention was riveted on them. As Beatrice approached him, with her friends trailing behind, the hunter drew back slightly, but he didn't retreat.

"Good morning, Orion," Beatrice said.

"I've been hoping to see you," the hunter said in a low voice.

Beatrice exchanged a surprised glance with Ollie.

"Why is that?" Ollie asked.

"I've learned from the gnomes that you went with them into the mines," Orion said. "Did you find a way to the top of the mountain?"

"Unfortunately, no," Beatrice said, but his question had triggered suspicion. "Why do you ask?"

He hesitated, and then he said, "Because I know another way."

Beatrice's pulse quickened. "To reach the top of Blood Mountain?" she asked. "But what about the giants and the birds of prey?"

Orion was leaning heavily on his crutch. He shifted his weight, grunting softly, and Beatrice realized that he must be in pain.

"There's a trail up the mountain that very few know about," the hunter said. "It's so narrow, the giants wouldn't be able to follow it—although they could lean down in some spots and grab you. As for the birds, you'd have to watch out for them and hide in among the rocks where they couldn't reach."

"Can we see the trail from here?" Teddy asked.

Orion shook his head. "It's hidden from the ground."

Beatrice was watching him closely, wishing that she could see the expression on his face. "How do *you* happen to know about it?"

"That doesn't matter," the hunter said, his voice deepening to a low rumble. He thrust a wrinkled sheet of parchment into her hand. "Here. I've drawn you a map. The trail starts about a hundred yards west of the mining tracks. You'll see three boulders set closely together. Go between the second and third, and you'll find the path."

He turned away, obviously intending to leave, but Beatrice still had questions. She reached out to stop him, and when her fingers brushed the arm of his robes, Orion jerked back in alarm.

"I—I'm sorry," Beatrice said hastily. "I just wanted to thank you, and ask why you're telling us this."

The hunter was silent for a moment before he said, "The witches of Winged-Horse Mountain have been kind to me, as have the gnomes. Perhaps I can help them by assisting you. I understand that you don't trust me," he added, "but the trail is your only chance of making it to the top of Blood Mountain. And you're still taking a great risk. Realize that before you decide what you're going to do."

Beatrice dropped her eyes to study the map, but something else caught her attention—something that made her gasp. Before she could speak, Orion turned around, surprisingly fast for a man who relied on a crutch, and disappeared into the darkness of the stables. This time, Beatrice didn't try to stop him. She was too busy contemplating what she had just seen.

"I'm not so sure about the trail," Teddy said. "We don't know anything about this guy. He could be setting us up."

"He could be," Beatrice agreed absently.

"But what other choice do we have?" Cyrus asked.

"None," Ollie replied. "I think we have to give it a shot."

"All right," Teddy said, "I'm game. When do we leave?"

"If we wait till dark," Ollie reasoned, "we'll stand a better chance of no one seeing us cross the desert to Blood Mountain."

"Beatrice?" Teddy was giving her a puzzled look. "You haven't said what you think."

Beatrice opened her mouth to speak, then stopped. She had almost blurted out her suspicions about Orion, but what if she was wrong about him? They had to make decisions based on what they knew, *not* what Beatrice suspected.

"If we're leaving tonight," Beatrice said, "I need to tell Miranda."

Teddy's expression was resigned.

After dinner, Beatrice and her friends went to their rooms to wait until it was time to leave. Beatrice pulled on jeans and hiking shoes. Then, on impulse, she reached for Dally Rumpe's spellbook, stuffed it into the pocket of a lightweight jacket, and tied the jacket around her waist.

Beatrice's hands were suddenly sweaty, and she rubbed them nervously on her jeaned legs. *Why am I taking the spellbook?* she wondered. She certainly didn't intend to use it. *Did she?*

17

Blood Mountain

hey left the ranch house, hoping that no one was watching, and started out across the dark desert. Remembering the intense heat on the mountain, Ollie had brought a backpack filled with bottles of water. Miranda had abandoned her Marco Bell disguise and was wearing stylish black pants, a black T-shirt, and black heelless shoes that didn't look very sturdy.

"You aren't exactly dressed for mountain climbing," Teddy commented as they headed toward the glowing red peaks of Blood Mountain. "Don't you have any hiking shoes?"

"You mean, like those ugly things you're wearing?" Miranda replied airily. "In a word—*no.*"

"I don't think the Ghumbabas care much about fashion," Teddy said hotly. "Who are you trying to impress, anyway?"

"There may be photographers when we come back heroes," Miranda answered. "I want to look my best."

"You won't even make it to the top of the mountain in those ridiculous shoes," Teddy muttered, "much less *come back a hero.*"

Beatrice privately agreed with Teddy, but she didn't

say anything. She just hoped that Miranda's vanity wouldn't put them in more danger than they already faced.

They skirted the mining carts and headed west around the base of the mountain, as Orion had instructed.

"There they are," Cyrus said a few moments later. "The boulders."

Three stones as tall as a two-story house rose out of the sand against the side of the mountain. Cayenne leaped from Beatrice's shoulder and darted into an opening between the second and third boulders.

"Cayenne," Beatrice hissed, "come back here! I don't want to lose sight of her," she said hastily, and squeezed through the opening herself.

The others followed, finding themselves on a rocky trail that wound up the side of the mountain. Once past the boulders, they could see that the path was cut into the rock, like the bed of a dry stream, its sides coming up past their waists and giving them a sense of protection. The giants and the birds would never be able to enter such a narrow space; but if a giant happened to be looking down, he would certainly see them from the cliffs above.

They saw at once that the climb was going to be difficult. The trail was steep and uneven, the air so hot and dry it seemed to scorch their nostrils when they inhaled. Beatrice struggled up the incline, mopping sweat from her face. It wasn't long before she had to stop to catch her breath. She called out Cayenne's name, and the cat sat down above her to wait.

Beatrice looked back at the others, just as Miranda slipped and landed hard on her hands. In the eery red light, Beatrice saw Miranda's face twist with pain. Ollie reached back to help Miranda, but the girl waved his hand away impatiently and scrambled to her feet on her own.

"Those stupid shoes," Teddy muttered as she reached Beatrice, and they exchanged a quick smile.

Beatrice peered over the side of the mountain while she and Teddy waited for the others.

"Look down there," Beatrice said, pointing to bones strewn across the rocks.

Teddy grimaced. "Are they human?"

"Looks like it."

Cyrus arrived panting and wiping his face on his sleeve, followed by Ollie and Miranda. Teddy stared pointedly at Miranda's shoes, one of which had already begun to separate from the sole. Miranda saw her looking and scowled.

"At this rate, it's going to take us all night," Ollie declared.

Just then, there was a crashing sound above them, then another—and the earth under their feet started to vibrate. Instinctively, they braced themselves against the rocky sides of the trail. Cayenne came tearing back to Beatrice and hid behind her mistress's legs.

"Earthquake!" Cyrus yelped.

"Uh-uh." Ollie shook his head grimly. "Giants walking!"

Beatrice threw her head back to look up. Sure enough, she saw three hideous Ghumbabas lumbering along the wide ledge in front of the mine entrance. Luckily, the giants didn't seem to have noticed Beatrice and her companions.

"Don't move!" Miranda hissed.

They all complied, hardly daring to breathe until the giants disappeared around the side of the mountain and the crashing sounds faded to dull thuds.

Teddy let out a quivering breath. "At least we'll know when they're nearby," she said.

Fifteen or twenty birds of prey were circling the top of the mountain. Suddenly, one swooped down toward the entrance to the tunnels, its powerful wings making a noise like muffled applause as they beat against the air. Beatrice was close enough to see that the bird was absolutely enormous—as large as a small horse—with gum-colored feathers stuck together in greasy clumps. Its black beak was at least two feet long, and so sharp that Beatrice had little doubt that it could pierce human flesh with no effort at all. The creature was grotesque, not to mention terrifying. Beatrice didn't move away from the mountain wall until the bird had flown back to join the others.

"We'd better get going," Ollie said hastily, "before the giants come back."

They continued up the narrow ravine, with Ollie leading this time, and were just below the ledge outside the mine entrance when Ollie slid on some loose rocks, sending a shower of pebbles down on Beatrice and the others. Someone yelled, "Ouch!"

Ollie paused long enough to say, "Sorry," before starting to climb again.

Just behind him, Beatrice felt the same pebbles rolling around under her feet and reached out to grab an outcrop of rock to steady herself. She saw something move only inches away from her fingers and jerked her hand back.

The brown scaly body of a snake was coiled on the rocks within striking distance of Beatrice's face. She found herself staring straight into the snake's hooded yellow eyes. Too startled to scream, Beatrice watched in silent terror as the reptile raised its head and opened its white-rimmed mouth, revealing sharp, venomous fangs.

Teddy saw the snake and let out a strangled cry. At the same moment, something came sailing through the air above Beatrice's shoulder. Thinking it was one of the birds, she ducked—then realized in horror that it was Cayenne who had flown past her. The cat had landed on the rocks less than a foot away from the snake, her puffed-up body arched like a Halloween cat.

Cayenne had drawn the reptile's attention away from Beatrice. Now the snake lifted its head and upper body into the air, preparing to strike the cat. Beatrice grabbed for her, but Cayenne was already leaping to Beatrice's shoulder—just missing the thrust of the snake's fangs by a hair.

"Let's get out of here!" Beatrice yelled, holding Cayenne protectively and beginning to scramble up the path as the snake made a slithering move toward them.

Pebbles scattered under their feet as they shoved and jostled one another in a frantic attempt to put distance between themselves and the snake. They didn't stop again until they were high above the mine entrance. Finally, exhausted from the heat and gasping for breath, they sank to the floor of the ravine.

Beatrice buried her face in Cayenne's fur. "You're such a brave girl," she crooned, her voice coming out in breathless spurts.

Miranda was watching Beatrice and Cayenne with interest. "That cat risked her life for you," Miranda said, and Beatrice thought she actually sounded impressed.

"This isn't the first time," Ollie said, reaching out to stroke Cayenne's head. "She's helped us every time we've come to the Sphere."

"I could use a cat like that," Miranda said.

Beatrice cut her eyes at Miranda. "Then you'll just have to find yourself one."

Staring steadily at Miranda, Cayenne meowed sharply, as if to say that she concurred.

After resting and drinking some water, they started out again. Occasionally, they heard the crashing sounds of giants close by—their cue to remain still until the noises faded away. They climbed for a long time, until Beatrice's legs were throbbing and her clothing was drenched with sweat. She was glad when Ollie suddenly stopped and pointed to a nearby formation of rock jutting out of the side of the mountain.

"It's the profile of Dally Rumpe's face," he said. "See the nose and the forehead? It looks like this trail goes behind his ear and up over his head."

"Then that means we're getting close to the top," Beatrice said.

"We're probably three-quarters there," Ollie replied.

"Well, I need to rest," Teddy said, and slumped against the mountain wall.

Beatrice watched as Miranda sat down and removed one of her shoes. It really was in ribbons now, with half the sole hanging loose. But Miranda didn't comment; she just emptied sand and pebbles out of the ruined shoe and put it back on.

"Could I have some more water?" Cyrus asked.

Ollie was reaching into his backpack for bottles of water when a large shadow passed over them, making them all look up.

Beatrice had expected to see one of the Ghumbabas peering down at them, but it wasn't a giant. It was the shadow of one of the birds of prey flying between them and the pulsing crimson sun. Suddenly, Beatrice realized that the bird had spotted them—and that it was diving straight for them!

"Everybody down!" Ollie shouted.

They hit the dirt, crouching together on the floor of the ravine. Beatrice was holding Cayenne tightly, hoping desperately that the bird wouldn't be able to get to them, when she noticed that Cyrus hadn't moved. He was still standing there, frozen with fear, his eyes glued to the swooping bird. And the bird was quite close now, just over Cyrus's head, with one leg—and those monstrous claws—extended toward him.

Beatrice passed Cayenne to Miranda and scrambled to her feet. She ran to Cyrus and grabbed hold of him to pull him down. But an instant later, the bird's sharp talons hooked themselves into Cyrus's shoulder, stabbing Beatrice's left hand. The pain shot up her arm like an electric current. All the blood drained from her face and her head started to swim.

Then everything went dark.

18

On Dally Rumpe's Head

Beatrice came to abruptly, conscious of a deafening noise and a burning pain in her hand. Her head was swimming, but then she remembered where she was and struggled to sit up.

She had fallen free from the bird's claw, but the creature still had Cyrus in its grip. Beatrice was vaguely aware of blood pouring from her hand and dripping to the ground. The noise, she realized, was the sound of the bird's flapping wings.

In a confused blur, Beatrice saw that Teddy and Miranda were clinging to each other, their faces frozen in terror. But what Ollie was doing didn't make sense at all. He was holding one of the water bottles up to the bird's face and screaming something that Beatrice couldn't hear over the sound of the beating wings.

Suddenly, the water in the bottle erupted like a small volcano—shooting straight into one of the bird's dark, glittering eyes. The creature's head jerked back, and from its beak came a terrible scream. As the bird loosened its hold on Cyrus, Beatrice understood what was happening.

Ollie had used his spell to blind the bird with boiling water. And it worked! Cyrus fell to the ground, while the bird lurched and wobbled in the air above their heads, in pain and apparently muddled by the attack.

Still feeling woozy and disconnected from everything around her, Beatrice was startled when Ollie suddenly yanked her to her feet.

"Run!" he shouted, and pointed toward Dally Rumpe's massive ear.

Then he released her and bent over Cyrus's prone body. Beatrice swayed unsteadily as she watched Ollie pull Cyrus from the ground. The shoulder of Cyrus's T-shirt was soaked with blood and his face was chalky.

Beatrice felt Teddy and Miranda's hands on her arms as they jerked her along the ravine. She staggered up the passageway, still dazed. They reached a prominent outcrop of stone that Beatrice realized must be Dally Rumpe's ear, and the path suddenly sloped down toward a crevice in the rock. Beatrice stumbled, and before she could catch herself, slid headfirst through the crevice and into a snug, dimly lit cavern. Teddy and Miranda hurried in after her, and moments later Ollie appeared, half carrying, half dragging Cyrus.

They crawled as far away from the cave's entrance as possible and huddled together. Beatrice could still hear the flapping of the bird's wings, but the sound was growing fainter. She hoped this meant that the creature was flying back to the top of the mountain.

Cyrus winced as Ollie pulled the T-shirt over his head.

"This doesn't look too bad," Ollie said, dabbing at the blood on Cyrus's shoulder. "Teddy, get a bottle of water and wash these wounds, okay?"

Then he crawled over to Beatrice and started examining her hand.

"There's one deep puncture," Ollie murmured, "but the bleeding's nearly stopped."

Ollie reached for another bottle of water and poured it over the wound. This made the pain worse, but Beatrice clenched her teeth and managed not to cry out. Ollie wiped the blood away with the hem of his shirt, then pulled a bandana from his pocket and tied it around her hand.

"How's that?" he asked her.

The burning pain had eased up a little. Beatrice flexed her fingers tentatively to make sure they still worked. "It's good, Ollie. Thanks."

Meanwhile, Teddy had cleaned Cyrus's shoulder and he was looking better. Some color had returned to his face, but even the smallest movement caused him to grimace in pain.

They all sat watching him for a few moments, and then Ollie said, "Cyrus, I don't think you're going to be able to climb."

Cyrus opened his mouth to protest, then shut it quickly. His glum expression told them that he knew Ollie was right.

"You should be safe here till we come back," Teddy said, her tone uncharacteristically gentle. She knew how much Cyrus hated being left behind.

"And Cayenne can stay with you," Beatrice added. "I'll feel better about her."

Now Ollie was looking at Beatrice. "What about you? Does your hand hurt too much to go on?"

It was still painful, and Beatrice wasn't sure how she was going to use the hand if she needed it for climbing. But if *she* didn't continue, there was no reason for the others to go on.

"It's fine," Beatrice said. "Hardly hurts at all."

Ollie gave her a skeptical look, but all he said was, "Okay then. If it gets worse, we'll just turn back."

They placed Ollie's backpack under Cyrus's head for him to use as a pillow and hooked Cyrus's belt to Cayenne's collar like a leash.

"You'll have to hold on to her," Beatrice said, handing the end of the belt to Cyrus. "She'll want to come with us."

"Don't worry, she'll be safe." Cyrus tried to smile, but he couldn't quite hide his disappointment.

"The birds and the giants can't get in here," Ollie said, "and if you see a spider, smack it with your shoe."

"We'll be back as soon as we can," Beatrice told him.

"Just be careful," Cyrus called after them as they left the cave.

Once back on the trail, Beatrice fell into step behind Teddy and Miranda, with Ollie coming last. Beatrice suspected that he was following behind to keep an eye on her.

She looked around warily. The birds were still circling the top of the mountain, but for the moment, they didn't seem to be paying any attention to the witches. She couldn't see any of the giants, but the earth vibrated as they stomped around somewhere nearby.

The trail was no longer cut into the mountain. It stood completely in the open—its travelers readily visible to anyone who was looking—curving around Dally Rumpe's ear and then rising sharply up the side of his head. Teddy and

Miranda grabbed hold of rocks to pull themselves up the steep incline, but Beatrice couldn't manage that with one hand. She had just decided that she was in big trouble when Ollie appeared beside her. Placing an arm firmly around her waist, he proceeded to lift her up the trail.

At this point, it was slow going for all of them; but, luckily, the path soon leveled off and began to wind across Dally Rumpe's forehead through the ridges of his hair. Beatrice began to feel more hopeful. Her hand was still aching, but as long as she didn't have to use it, she thought she might make it. Her optimism, however, was premature.

Just as they came to Dally Rumpe's left eyebrow, Beatrice felt the earth tremble. Then came that sound— the crash of giants' feet on the mountain.

"Oh, gosh," Teddy gasped. "There they are!"

Teddy and Miranda had come to an abrupt stop and were looking down. Beatrice peered in the same direction and saw two giants coming around the other side of Dally Rumpe's head. They were lumbering along on the stone ledge that was supposed to be the sorcerer's collar, but the Ghumbabas were so tall, their hideous veined heads were only a few feet below the witches' feet. Beatrice was thinking that, at least, it didn't appear that the Ghumbabas had seen them, when one of the giants looked up.

It took a moment for the witches' presence to register, but then the giant's glistening mouth fell open and there was a faint glint in his dull eyes. He grunted, getting his companion's attention, and soon the mean, squinting eyes of two giants were focused on Beatrice and her companions.

"Maybe we can back up," Teddy said quickly.

"It's too late for that," Miranda snapped.

"Then what do you suggest?" Teddy burst out, sounding on the verge of panic.

One of the giants had lifted his hand into the air, as if he meant to grab them. Miranda, who was closest to his enormous, grimy fist, jumped out of the way, nearly knocking Teddy over.

Beatrice saw that Miranda was right. They wouldn't have time to make it back across Dally Rumpe's forehead; the Ghumbabas would just reach up and crush them—or knock them off the side of the mountain with their clubs. The giants were moving slowly toward them even now.

In desperation, Beatrice began to chant:

> Circle of magic, hear my pleas,
> Send lightning down
> On our enemies.
> This, I ask you, do for me.

All at once, they heard a rumble of thunder. Black clouds rolled in across the red sun, and a jagged spear of lightning shot down from the clouds. It struck with a loud cracking sound at the giants' feet.

The giants stumbled back, startled but too stupid to react quickly. Another bolt hit the ledge and the giants moved backward again—into thin air. A look of vague surprise came over their faces as they fell from the mountain.

Beatrice couldn't watch. She turned away and Ollie slid an arm around her shoulders.

"Way to go, Cuz!" Miranda exclaimed.

But Beatrice was thoroughly shaken and didn't reply. She leaned back against Dally Rumpe's eyebrow and wiped the sweat from her face.

"We'd better get going," Ollie said, frowning as he peered at the birds still circling overhead.

The others followed him quickly to the other side of Dally Rumpe's head. At this point, the trail became steep again, winding over the top of the sorcerer's skull.

Teddy grabbed hold of Beatrice's good hand and pulled her up the path, while Ollie pushed against Beatrice's back. This was the hardest part of the climb so far. Teddy and Ollie kept slipping and falling to the ground, the sharp rocks cutting through the knees of their jeans. Beatrice caught sight of Miranda's feet and noticed that there were bloody gashes above her cousin's ripped and battered shoes.

Inch by painful inch, they continued up the side of the mountain—until, finally, they were standing on top of Dally Rumpe's head.

"I can't believe we made it," Teddy said, bending over with her hands pressed to her thighs while she tried to catch her breath.

Shading her eyes from the blinding red sun, Beatrice squinted up at the one peak remaining to be climbed. "Another thirty-five or forty feet and we're there," she said, noting that the birds of prey seemed to have all collected around that peak, no doubt waiting for the witches' arrival.

Miranda was looking out across the desert, and following her gaze, Beatrice realized that they could see the ranch house from here. It appeared no larger than a child's dollhouse, nestled in the shade of Winged-Horse Mountain.

"If I ever get back there," Miranda said dreamily, "I'm going to take a three-hour bubble bath and eat a gallon of ice cream."

"*After* you get those feet attended to," Beatrice said.

Miranda glanced down at her bruised and bloodied feet. "I guess Teddy was right about the shoes," she admitted, sounding almost good-natured.

Teddy stared at Miranda with her mouth hanging open.

Just then, Ollie turned sharply toward a peak some twenty feet away. Sensing his tension, Beatrice looked in that direction and saw another giant standing there watching them. *He's not close enough to grab us*, Beatrice thought. But then she saw that he was swinging something over his head. It was a lariat!

"He's going to try to catch us," Ollie said before Beatrice could speak.

Teddy was looking around for someplace to hide, but they were in the open, without so much as a rock or a bush to crouch behind.

"Okay, my turn," Miranda said.

Beatrice, Teddy, and Ollie watched in bewilderment as Miranda limped to the edge of the plateau and faced the giant. They understood when she began to chant:

> *Spirits of the earth and sea,*
> *This, I ask you, do for me:*
> *Take the lariat from his hand,*
> *So it won't work the way he planned.*

They watched as the rope was torn from the giant's hands by some unseen force and then hurled over the side of the mountain. The giant just stared after the lariat, his face completely blank.

Beatrice grinned at Miranda. "Pretty fancy spellwork," she said.

"What kind of spell was that, anyway?" Teddy wanted to know.

"A make-things-not-work-properly spell," Miranda answered with a smug half smile. Then the smile faltered. "It's the only kind of spell I can work," she admitted.

"Welcome to the club," Teddy said cheerfully.

Miranda smiled again, but this time, there was nothing smug about it.

19

Drude the Terrible

They climbed in silence for the next half hour, staying as close to the mountain wall as possible, and always conscious of the birds flying overhead. The path was nearly straight up now, and it was only by sheer determination that they managed to inch along toward the summit. At times, they were forced to crawl on their hands and knees. Beatrice had to support her weight with her one good arm and hop along like a dog with an injured paw.

As they drew closer to the top of Blood Mountain, Beatrice's mind was working overtime. How were they going to get past the birds of prey? They couldn't just pop up over the edge and expect the birds to ignore them. And once at the top, who knew how far they'd have to go to reach Morven?

They stopped to rest, and Beatrice looked up to gauge how much farther they had to climb. Only ten or twelve feet more. For the first time, she noticed a shallow overhang of stone jutting out from the mountain. If they stayed close to the cliff wall, the birds wouldn't be able to see them—at least, not until they reached the top and stepped out into the open.

They started climbing again, the overhang not only protecting them from view but also shading them from the red sun. Finally, Beatrice could see that the trail leveled off just above her head, disappearing behind a pile of boulders on top of the mountain.

Everyone moved cautiously up the final few feet of the path. Still in the lead, Teddy and Miranda reached the boulders first.

Teddy turned back to Beatrice, looking excited. "It's like another cave," she whispered.

Sure enough, when Beatrice crept into the cluster of huge stones, she saw that there was a natural bridge of rock overhead, shielding them from the birds.

"Not a bad place to hide while we get our bearings," Ollie said, and crawled into the tight space with the girls.

"Look over there," Miranda said, pointing.

Through an opening in the boulders, they could see that the mountaintop was essentially flat, and perched on the opposite edge was a small adobe house.

"That must be where he's keeping Morven," Beatrice said softly.

"So how do we get there?" Miranda asked, frowning as she studied the open space between them and their destination.

A few of the birds were flying over Morven's house, and Beatrice's throbbing hand was a vivid reminder of the damage they could do. She started thinking hard.

"You could do some kind of weather spell to divert the birds' attention," Ollie said to Beatrice. "Hail, maybe. Except we'd be in the middle of it, too,"

"*Or*," Teddy said, turning to Miranda, "you could make the birds' wings not work or something."

"Afraid not," Miranda said. "The spell only works on inanimate objects."

"Well, there has to be *something* we can do," Ollie insisted. "We're so close now."

But after thinking for a long time, no one came up with anything.

Beatrice was chewing her bottom lip nervously. There *was* one way . . . But would she do it? Did she *want* to do it?

"You've come up with something," Ollie said, watching Beatrice's face. "Tell us."

Reluctantly, Beatrice untied the sleeves of her jacket from around her waist and reached into the pocket. When she withdrew Dally Rumpe's spellbook, Teddy's eyes opened wide.

"But I thought—" Teddy started.

"You planned to use it all along?" Miranda cut in, eyebrows raised.

"No," Beatrice said firmly. "I just—brought it. I'm not sure why. It was a last-minute decision."

"Well, since you have it here," Miranda said, "and it looks like there's no other way . . ."

Ollie was staring into Beatrice's face, his brow furrowed. "Don't do it," he said quietly. "I know you, Beatrice. Even if it worked, you'd never feel good about it."

Beatrice was practically glaring at the book in her hands. Ollie was right, but what else were they supposed to do? Just give up and head back down the mountain? And who was to say they'd even *make* it down?

"I don't know what else to do," Beatrice said help-lessly. "I mean, we're already in a fix—and we haven't even seen that bird that guards Morven yet."

"Oh, yeah, Drude," Teddy said. "I'd forgotten about him."

Beatrice hadn't taken her eyes off the book. Now she opened it, her hands trembling.

"I guess we could just see if there's a spell that might help us," she said, and then stopped as a folded sheet of yellowed parchment fell from the back of the book and floated to the ground.

Beatrice reached down to pick it up.

"What is that?" Teddy asked.

"It looks like a letter," Beatrice replied as she unfolded the parchment. "A very *old* letter. It's addressed to Dally Rumpe—or, actually, to Dalbert, before he *became* Dally Rumpe."

Teddy, Miranda, and Ollie were looking at the letter with keen interest.

"So read it," Miranda said.

"'*Dalbert,*'" Beatrice read, "'*I know that my time on this earth is short, and I have been giving much thought to what I will leave my sons. As the elder son, you fully expect to inherit all that I possess, including Bailiwick, but I have decided that your brother is more deserving of this than you. Furthermore, I believe that I would be doing you a disservice if I didn't try one last time to make a man of you. Therefore, I am leaving every-thing to Bromwich except this book. I can almost see your face as you read this, with all the anger and greed I have witnessed there so often before, but my gift to you is more valuable than you might imagine. There is great power in these spells. The fact* that there is also great evil only strengthens my belief that this is an appropriate bequest for you. I have watched you grow from a nasty and lazy child to a nastier and lazier adult, and I believe it is now too late for you to become a decent man. But it is not too late for you to become an accomplished one. Take this book and study it diligently. Perhaps there is still time for you to make something of yourself. I had high expectations for you, boy, but you've let me down more times than I can count. I'm gravely disappointed in you.'"

Beatrice looked up. "It's signed 'Lazarus Bailiwick.'"

"I didn't even notice the letter when I was reading the spells," Ollie said.

"I guess we never looked inside the back cover," Beatrice replied.

"Your grandfather told us that Dally Rumpe's father left him nothing but the spellbook," Teddy said to Miranda. "Now I understand why. It sounds like Dally Rumpe was always a loser."

"Still, this letter is pretty harsh," Beatrice said. "Dally Rumpe's father was *encouraging* him to become evil. It's as if he thought being a monster was better than being a failure."

Beatrice frowned, looking down at the letter. Some of these words sounded awfully familiar. She had heard them somewhere . . . somewhere recently. And then she remembered. She knew *exactly* where she had heard the words!

Beatrice was about to tell the others when Miranda suddenly gripped her arm. Staring at Morven's house, Miranda said, "Look!"

Beatrice looked, and what she saw made her heart start to pound. It was Drude—there was no doubt about that. The bird was standing near the house—it was almost as *large* as the house—peering around with its glittering eyes as if looking for something. The other birds were awful, but Drude was much more terrible! His feathers were an oily gray color, but clumps of them were missing all over his body, revealing raw pinkish flesh that seemed to be oozing pus. As the bird's head turned on his long, scrawny neck, more feathers floated to the ground. And then the odor reached Beatrice's nose—a stench that made her think of rotting meat left out in the sun. It had to be coming from Drude, and even this far away, the smell was revolting!

Teddy made a gagging sound and then clamped her hand over her nose.

"Hideous!" Miranda exclaimed. "How are we supposed to confront *that?* Beatrice, start looking for a spell in that book."

"Wait a minute," Ollie said quickly. "What's he doing?"

Drude was walking slowly away from the house, his long bowed legs appearing too skinny to support his ponderous body. Besides being disgusting, he looked ridiculous.

He kept walking, his eyes raised skyward. Then suddenly he made a screeching sound that was so loud Beatrice and her companions cringed. The birds overhead responded at once. They began to fly lower, heading in Drude's direction.

"He's calling them in," Ollie said. "I wonder why."

"Maybe they've reported seeing us," Teddy suggested, "and he's checking on our whereabouts."

Now all the birds were on the ground, looking relatively small as they milled around the enormous Drude.

"He's moved pretty far away from the house," Beatrice said, "and they aren't paying attention to anything but one another. Should we make a run for it?"

Miranda looked steadily at her. "You aren't going to use the book?"

Beatrice hesitated, then stuffed the spellbook back into the pocket of her jacket. "Dally Rumpe never should have used it," she said, "and neither should I."

"Too soft," Miranda muttered, and shook her head.

"If we're going, we'd better do it now," Teddy said. She glanced at Miranda's battered feet. "Maybe you should sit this one out."

"Not a chance," Miranda answered.

They all turned back to look at the birds, who were still standing together some distance away.

"On the count of three, run as fast as you've ever run in your life," Ollie said. "One. Two. Three."

The four came bursting out from the pile of boulders and started racing across the mountaintop. Focused solely on reaching the house, no one was watching the birds. But halfway there, Beatrice heard the sound of beating wings. Still running, she jerked her head around in time to see most of the smaller birds take to the sky. Drude hadn't left the ground, but he was flapping his great wings and watching them.

"They've seen us!" Beatrice shouted as Drude lifted off the ground.

Beatrice knew there was no way they could outrun the monstrous birds—especially Drude. In seconds, the whole menacing flock was directly over the witches. Wads of Drude's feathers were falling across the landscape like flakes of filthy snow, and the air was permeated with his disgusting odor. Then something heavier than a feather fell to the ground in front of them. A *stick*, Beatrice thought, wondering in confusion if the birds had started throwing things at them. But then she noticed the bright feathers sticking up out of the sand and realized that it was an arrow.

Beatrice looked around in bewilderment, and was startled to see another arrow zooming toward the underbelly of one of the birds. And then another, and another. The arrows were no more than pinpricks to the gigantic creatures, but even so, the steady barrage was having an effect. The cluster of birds above the witches' heads had broken up. They seemed to be unsettled by the attack and were now flying around aimlessly. Even Drude's attention was no longer centered on Beatrice and the others; the bird was staring beyond them to the edge of the mountaintop.

But who—? Beatrice stopped running and turned around, looking for whoever was shooting the arrows. Ollie, Teddy, and Miranda halted, too, gasping for breath as their eyes searched the landscape.

Then Beatrice saw him. Standing in front of one of the boulders was a figure in a hooded cloak, his bow releasing yet another arrow into the sky. It was Orion!

Beatrice had never been more grateful to see anyone—although she knew that he wouldn't be able to hold Drude off for long. And, meanwhile, he was putting himself in danger.

"Orion!" Beatrice shouted. "Go back!"

The hunter raised a hand in greeting, then motioned for her to continue on. And placing another arrow into his bow, he shot it at Drude.

"He can hide in the pile of boulders," Ollie said, "and probably a dozen other places. Orion knows this mountain, remember?"

Then Ollie grabbed Beatrice's hand and started sprinting toward the house. Teddy and Miranda sped after them.

The house sat on the opposite edge of the mountaintop from Orion. As they drew near, Beatrice saw that it was *right* on the edge. She was heading straight for the door—hoping it was unlocked—hoping Orion would get away—when she heard the roar of beating wings overhead. The mountain trembled as Drude suddenly landed between the witches and the house.

For an instant, Beatrice was staring directly into the dark beady eyes of the bird. Then he lifted one enormous wing, and Beatrice knew immediately what he was going to do. It happened so swiftly, she didn't even have time to feel afraid. With one great sweep, the bird's wing struck Beatrice and her companions, knocking them over the side of the mountain.

20

High Expectations

T he red cliffs flashed past her eyes as Beatrice plummeted to earth. She reached out instinctively, grabbing for something to hold on to, but her hands grasped only empty air.

Someone screamed. *Teddy or Miranda*, Beatrice thought, but she was too stunned to react. And then, just as she expected to crash into the rocks at the bottom of the mountain, Beatrice's body landed on something—but it wasn't stone. Her hands made contact with something warm and scratchy. Something alive! Beatrice wrapped her arms around the solid warmth and realized that she was no longer falling, but was soaring upward toward the mountaintop.

It took a few seconds for Beatrice to take in what was happening—to grasp the fact that she was straddling Balto's broad back and holding on for dear life to his massive neck.

Hands were digging into the flesh at Beatrice's waist. She twisted around and caught a glimpse of Teddy pressed against her back, and Miranda squeezed in behind Teddy. And there was Ollie, lying facedown over Balto's flanks, his arms clamped around the horse's body and his legs flying out over the white silky tail like a banner.

Beatrice felt a dizzying relief. But she barely had time to absorb the reality of their rescue before the horse flew up over the top of the mountain, and once again, Morven's house came into view.

Beatrice saw that the birds of prey were still circling. And there was Drude—hovering over the house, dropping clumps of greasy feathers across the roof.

Balto sailed in and landed near the house. He bent down to let the riders know it was time to dismount. Beatrice and her companions slid from his back, but their feet had barely touched the ground when Drude came diving toward them.

Beatrice turned frantically to Balto, thinking he would carry them away again. But the horse seemed to have no intention of fleeing. He was staring defiantly at the enormous bird, snorting as he pounded the earth with his front hoof.

Drude's immense shadow covered them, and Beatrice's head jerked up in panic. The bird was so close she could see his eyes glittering with fury as he thrust his gnarled claws toward them.

Balto was still pawing the ground. Suddenly thunder rumbled overhead and a jagged spear of lightning struck just in front of Drude. The bird pulled sharply upward and let out a horrible screech. Beatrice and the other witches took advantage of the moment and started running for the door of Morven's house.

The shadow fell over them again as they raced up the steps. Beatrice grabbed the doorknob and jerked the door open. With Drude's wings beating in their ears, the witches dashed inside and slammed the door shut behind them.

Beatrice leaned against the wall, panting as her eyes darted around the small room. She saw a dining table in the center and two armchairs near the fireplace. And in a doorway on the far side of the room stood a young woman with long, red-gold hair.

"Morven?" Beatrice said quickly.

The woman nodded. "Who are you?" she asked, eyeing Beatrice warily.

"That," came a high voice from behind Morven, "is the famous Beatrice Bailiwick."

Morven's head snapped toward the voice. She was obviously frightened. Then she looked back at Beatrice, her eyes very large. "Bailiwick," Morven whispered. "You've come—?"

"To *save* you," said the voice with a snicker.

And then someone Beatrice had been expecting brushed past Morven and stepped into the room.

"I don't believe it," Teddy murmured, looking shocked.

"*You?*" Miranda exclaimed with a disgusted expression.

"Me," said Kasper Cloud calmly, his dark eyes piercing each of their faces until finally coming to rest on Beatrice's.

The idea of this small handsome boy being the evil sorcerer was disconcerting, even though Beatrice had suspected that Kasper and Dally Rumpe were one in the same.

"I knew it was you," she said.

Kasper's eyes narrowed. "I don't believe you," he said softly. "You thought I was just a poor little boy with neglectful parents."

"At first I did," Beatrice admitted. "But then we found your spellbook—and the letter from your father."

Kasper's face darkened with anger, and he no longer looked either young *or* handsome. "I have no father," he said coldly.

Beatrice blew her bangs aside and willed herself to stay calm.

"That day Seamus took us on the walking tour you said something that I thought was very sad," Beatrice told him. "You repeated something your father had supposedly said to you. 'I have high expectations of you, boy, but you've let me down more times than I can count. I'm gravely disappointed in you.'"

Kasper's eyes flickered ominously.

"Those were the same words we read in Lazarus Bailiwick's letter to his son," Beatrice went on evenly. "That's when I knew that Kasper Cloud was really Dalbert Bailiwick."

"Dalbert Bailiwick no longer exists," he hissed.

And before their eyes, Kasper began to change. He was growing taller, and his round boyish face started to lengthen. The blood seemed to drain from his cheeks, leaving a grayish pallor, while the skin stretched tightly over his jaw and cheekbones until his head resembled a skull.

Beatrice and the others watched in horrified fascination. They had witnessed this change before, but seeing a human face become that of a monster was something they hadn't gotten used to.

Dally Rumpe's dark eyes were sunk back in his bony head, but they still glittered with malevolence. Beatrice realized now that she had been holding on to the faint hope that Dally Rumpe might still possess some small shred of conscience—that she might be able to reach the part of him that remained human. But she could see *nothing* human in this evil face.

"So you thought you could cast my spells," the evil sorcerer said, his voice deep and raspy. He flashed Beatrice a hideous grin. "I enchanted that book so that you would *think* you were casting the spells on your own. Of course, I made sure they'd never work on me—or any of my loyal followers."

Strangely enough, considering their predicament, Beatrice felt relieved. So she wasn't able to cast his evil spells, after all!

Dally Rumpe's black eyes stabbed her face. "But the fact that you wouldn't even *try* to use my spells against me confirms what I already knew. You're spineless, Beatrice Bailiwick. And *you!*" he snarled, turning to Miranda. "You could have had it all—but you sided with this poor excuse for a witch instead, and now look at you. You're pathetic!"

"We all have choices to make," Miranda said, her voice admirably steady, "and I don't regret mine."

At that, Dally Rumpe laughed, a cold, hollow sound that made Beatrice shiver. She watched as he pulled a small leather pouch from inside his robes and turned it upside down. Dozens of rubies spilled out on the table.

"This is what you could have had," Dally Rumpe said slyly to Miranda. "I'm growing richer every day."

Miranda's chin rose a fraction and she glared at the sorcerer.

Obviously angered by her defiant composure, Dally Rumpe began to sweep the rubies back into their bag.

"I've wasted enough time on you witches," he snarled, his eyes smouldering. "*Outside!* Drude and his friends are waiting for you!"

Dally Rumpe reached behind him for a mining pick and used it to prod them toward the door. As Beatrice stepped outside into the red shimmering heat, she glanced back and saw that Morven was following hesitantly behind Dally Rumpe.

The birds circled in tight formation overhead. A short distance away, Drude was waiting on the ground.

Beatrice's mind was working furiously. Should they run for it? They couldn't possibly move faster than Dally Rumpe or Drude, but Beatrice wasn't about to just stand there and let that nasty bird pluck them up like trembling lambs. She stole a glance at Dally Rumpe, and the look of triumph on his grotesque face was more than she could bear. Anger exploded inside her chest. So what if Dally Rumpe had them this time? They didn't have to make it *easy* for him!

"Run!" Beatrice screamed.

It was as if the others had just been waiting to hear this. Without hesitation, Teddy, Miranda, and Ollie began to sprint across the mountaintop behind Beatrice.

Beatrice heard Dally Rumpe's shriek of rage and then the furious beating of Drude's wings as he took to the air. She looked over her shoulder and saw that the sorcerer was just standing there, shouting oaths at them, but the monstrous bird was flying after them. And then she saw Morven, her brilliant hair blowing out behind her as she ran with Beatrice and the other witches.

Beatrice felt a burst of courage. Morven could have stayed safely behind, but she was coming with them. Still running as hard as she could, Beatrice found herself grinning. She grabbed hold of Morven's hand, and between ragged breaths, began to chant:

> By the power of the west,
> By the beauty of the light,
> Release this circle, I do implore,
> Make all that's wrong revert to right.

The sound of beating wings moved closer. Beatrice continued to chant:

> By the power of the west,
> By the spirit of the wood,
> Release this circle, I do implore,
> Make all that's evil revert to good.

Drude's shadow touched them, and still, Beatrice chanted:

> By the power of the west,
> By the chant of witch's song,
> Release this circle, I do implore,
> Make all that's weak revert to strong.

Beatrice's legs were beginning to feel rubbery, and she was too breathless to continue the spell. Then she felt the stirring of air as Drude swooped lower, flying just above them. With feathers falling over her head and shoulders, the bird's horrible stench nearly smothering her, Beatrice realized that time was running out. At any moment, she would feel those painful claws slice into her.

Unable to run any longer, Beatrice came to a stumbling halt, as did her panting companions. They were leaning against one another, trying to catch their breath, when Beatrice caught sight of something whizzing through the sky. She threw her head back and was nearly blinded by the crimson sun. But then, blinking furiously, she saw him. Balto had come back!

Beatrice's eyes darted to Drude. He was hovering in the air just above them, but his attention had been diverted by the horse. Balto seemed to be flying at a remarkable speed—straight for Drude's head. The horse zoomed in, his hooves level with the bird's eyes, when Drude pulled up sharply. Balto flew past, made a quick turn, and started back.

Beatrice heard a shout, and her eyes dropped to the ground. It was Dally Rumpe, running toward them as he waved the mining pick in the air.

Still breathing in short, shallow spurts, Beatrice forced out the words.

By the power of the west,
By the goodness of the dove,
Release this circle, I do implore,
Make all that's hateful revert to love.

Heed this charm, attend to me,
As my word, so mote it be!

Beatrice turned to Dally Rumpe, who had stopped running and was standing only a few feet away as if frozen in place. The mining pick fell from his hand with a dull thud. For an instant, Beatrice's eyes locked with his, and she felt the full force of his hatred and rage. Then he fell to the ground, screeching and writhing in pain.

Drude and the other birds of prey had disappeared. The crimson sun had vanished. Off to the east, the real sun was rising above the horizon, spreading a golden glow across the desert and over the ordinary, sand-colored stone of Blood Mountain. Beatrice looked around in wonder, and then her eyes returned to Dally Rumpe.

The sorcerer's body was evaporating into a cloud of mist. A gentle breeze ruffled Beatrice's hair, and as she watched, it carried the mist out across the desert.

Morven approached Beatrice, her face radiant.

"Thank you," Morven said fervently. "I had given up hope of ever being free. And my sisters?" she added, an anxious frown creasing her brow. "My father?"

"Your father is still held captive," Beatrice said, "but Rhona, Innes, and Ailsa have all been freed."

Morven looked as if she hardly dared believe this. "Then I can see them?"

"They'll probably be on their way here very soon," Ollie said gently. "Word seems to travel fast around the Sphere."

"And Dally Rumpe will never be able to return to Blood Mountain?" Morven asked, her voice trembling slightly.

"Never," Beatrice answered.

She was suddenly aware of the steady throbbing in her hand and of feeling very tired. She looked around at Teddy, Miranda, and Ollie. They all looked pleased. And exhausted.

"We'd better start back," Beatrice said. "Cyrus and Cayenne will wonder what's happened to us."

"Will I see you again?" Morven asked. She paused, then added timidly, "Perhaps at my father's castle?"

Beatrice wished that her association with Dally Rumpe and his ghouls could end right now. But she had committed herself to one more trip to the Witches' Sphere.

"We promised to help your father," Beatrice said, "so we'll be back."

Meanwhile, Miranda had been searching the sky and scowling.

"Where is that demented horse?" she muttered. "I was hoping for a ride back to the ranch."

Beatrice grinned. Then she looked down at Miranda's bloody feet and her amusement faded.

"I'm sorry I distrusted you," Beatrice said.

"I take your suspicion as a positive sign," Miranda said crisply. "You're altogether too nice—not to mention, gullible. It's time for a master to take you in hand and toughen you up."

"And you're the master, I suppose," Teddy retorted.

Miranda folded her arms across her chest and looked steadily at Teddy. "Do you know a badder witch than me?" she asked.

21

The Bailiwick Ruby

As they made their way back down Blood Mountain, Beatrice glanced over her shoulder, listening for the heavy footfalls of the Ghumbabas. But like Dally Rumpe, Drude, and the other birds of prey, the giants were gone.

Cyrus and Cayenne were waiting for them outside the cave.

Beatrice scooped up a delighted Cayenne and said to Cyrus, "Should you be walking around?"

"I'm feeling better," Cyrus answered, "just sore. But not knowing what was happening was awful—and we heard a scream!" Cyrus's eyes had grown large and round, but suddenly he grinned. "Then Cayenne looked out and came back all excited, talking a mile a minute. I knew you'd broken the spell when I followed her outside—because Blood Mountain wasn't red anymore!"

"Balto, Orion, and Miranda saved our lives," Teddy added casually, making a point of not looking at Miranda.

Cyrus glanced at Teddy to see if she was serious, then turned curious eyes on Miranda, whose expression was unreadable.

"Come on," Beatrice said, smiling at his bewilderment. "We'll tell you all about it—but I've had enough of this mountain for one day."

It wasn't long before they reached the end of the trail and emerged from the boulders at the mountain's base. Balto and Orion were waiting nearby. The hunter was leaning on his crutch, his face still hidden beneath the hood. Beside him, the winged horse appeared uncharacteristically tranquil, his white coat gleaming in the morning sun.

Hurrying toward them, Beatrice said, "Thank you—both of you. We never would have made it without you."

"I didn't do much," Orion said gruffly. "I'm just glad that someone was finally able to make it to the top of that mountain."

"You tried it a year ago, didn't you?" Beatrice asked gently.

Orion's body tensed, and Beatrice's friends gave her puzzled looks.

"Is there something you haven't told us?" Miranda asked, giving her cousin a penetrating look.

"It's not my place to tell you," Beatrice replied, still looking at Orion.

There was a long silence, and finally the hunter said quietly, "How did you know?"

Beatrice's eyes dropped to his throat, where a gold chain glinted above the collar of his robes.

"I see," Orion said.

He reached for the chain, and as they watched, pulled out a gold medallion. The ruby in its center glowed a rich red in the sun.

"Joy told you?" Orion asked.

Beatrice nodded. "She said she gave you the medallion for your birthday. Then I caught a glimpse of it under your robes when you were telling us about the hidden trail."

Ollie's eyebrows shot up. "You're Dominy Griffin!"

The hunter shifted uneasily.

"But everyone thinks you're dead," Teddy blurted out. "Why—?"

"You don't owe us an explanation," Beatrice said quickly.

Dominy sighed. "I think I do," he said.

With a quick motion, he swept the hood back from his face, revealing thick russet hair—and a face so badly scarred that Beatrice would never have recognized him as the handsome young man in the photograph.

"The birds did that?" Beatrice asked softly.

Dominy nodded. "I took the same path you did and was nearly to the top when they swooped down on me, clawing at my back and shoulders. And my face."

Beatrice's gaze followed the pink ropes of scar tissue that ran across his forehead, down his nose and cheekbones, to his jaw. There were deep gouges on one side of his face, so that his cheek appeared sunken, and his mouth was pulled down at one corner. Only his brilliant blue eyes had been left untouched.

"But you escaped with your life," Beatrice murmured.

"Just," Dominy said. "One bird picked me up and dropped me onto the rocks, breaking my ribs and collarbone and one of my legs. I was still conscious and able to crawl into a cave out of their reach. Eventually, I healed. But—" he paused, spreading his hands wide in a gesture of resignation, "how could I go back to Joy and my father? Like this."

"They wouldn't care," Beatrice said promptly, certain that this was true. "Losing you has been terrible for them, Dominy."

His eyes clouded with sorrow, Dominy said, "I know. I've watched them. I've even thought . . ."

"Of going back?" Miranda asked when he didn't finish.

Beatrice glanced quickly at Miranda, surprised by the kindness she heard in her cousin's voice.

"Yes," Dominy replied. "But I was—afraid. Look at me!" he demanded, his voice suddenly bitter. "Why should Joy be stuck with a—a—monster?"

"I don't think you're giving her enough credit," Beatrice said. "And, anyway, shouldn't she be able to make up her own mind? Come back with us. See for yourself how Joy reacts. If she's the witch I think she is, this will be the happiest day of her life."

"I—I can't," he said, and jerked the hood back over his face.

Beatrice started to say something else, but Dominy was already limping away toward Blood Mountain. As he disappeared behind the boulders, Beatrice shouted, "Please, Dominy—just give it a chance!"

"You've done all you can do," Ollie said quietly to Beatrice. "You can't force him to go back."

"But it's such a *waste!*" Beatrice cried out.

About that time, she felt a nudge at her elbow. Beatrice turned to find Balto standing there, gently nuzzling her arm.

"It's nice to finally meet you, too," Beatrice said, reaching out to stroke the horse's silky mane. "And thank you for saving us."

Balto whinnied softly.

Shaking her head, Miranda muttered, "Some wild horse he is. Honestly, Beatrice, you've turned him into a pussy cat."

Cayenne cut her eyes at Miranda as if to say, *And what's wrong with that?*

Beatrice and her companions started across the desert for Winged-Horse Ranch, with Cayenne riding blissfully on Balto's back. As they approached the front gates, Beatrice saw that a large welcoming committee had gathered outside. All the campers—with one noticeable exception—were there, as well as a great number of gnomes. Chaucer and O. Henry were jumping up and down, Dickens was turning cartwheels, and even Longfellow was grinning from ear to ear. Beatrice caught sight of Seamus and Joy, and she wished even more fervently that she had been able to convince Dominy to come home. Paxton was there, as was Ira Skelly, who was practically glued to Joy, and Uri stood nearby with Fairlamb and Winifred Stoop. When the travelers walked through the front gates, the excited crowd burst into applause.

Her face turning pink, Beatrice said under her breath, "This is always the worst part."

"Why is everyone staring at me?" Miranda muttered. Then, with a hint of panic in her voice, she burst out, "They're going to arrest me! I've got to get out of here."

Beatrice looked around and realized that a lot of curious and expectant eyes did seem to be focused on her cousin.

"Maybe it's because they haven't seen you out of your Marco Bell disguise," Beatrice whispered back, "and they're wondering who you are."

"I don't think that's it," Miranda answered nervously, and then stopped short.

Xenos Bailiwick had stepped out from the crowd. The applause died, and every eye was trained on Xenos as he started toward Miranda.

"Uh-oh," Teddy murmured. She took hold of Miranda's arm and said stoutly, "We'll just tell them that you risked your life for us—that we couldn't have broken the spell without you."

Miranda gave Teddy an astonished look, and then turned her attention back to her grandfather.

Xenos stopped in front of her.

"You're smiling," Miranda said, eyeing him with suspicion.

"And why shouldn't I be?" Xenos asked, his dark eyes shining. "This is a fine day for the Witches' Sphere—and for the Bailiwick family. My granddaughter, my great-niece, and their three brave friends have come back from Blood Mountain. As heroes, I might add."

Miranda blinked. "But I'm a—fugitive!"

Xenos was still smiling. "Not anymore," he said placidly. "I've just spoken with the authorities. Word of Dally Rumpe's defeat has already spread across the Sphere—including the part you played in it, Miranda. The warrant for your arrest has been rescinded."

Miranda appeared dazed. "Are you sure? Just like that?" Then her eyes narrowed. "But I'll have to go back to that reform school, right?"

"No, Miranda," Xenos said. "When I sent you to The Rightpath School, I told you that you could come home as soon as I was sure that you'd really changed. Well, I'm sure," he added softly. "You showed great loyalty to your cousin and her friends."

Xenos glanced at Beatrice, as if for confirmation, and Beatrice said hastily, "She did, Uncle Xenos. She saved our lives."

Xenos placed one arm around Beatrice's shoulders and the other around Miranda's. "I must say, you girls—and all of you," he said, his eyes moving to include Teddy, Ollie, and Cyrus, "have made me very proud. Now—I believe they've planned a party for you all, in honor of your victory. Shall we go inside and do some serious celebrating?"

"What about Balto?" Beatrice asked.

"Morven sent word that she's coming for him," Joy said, gazing with affection at the white horse. "Longfellow can care for him till then."

The gnome stepped forward, obviously delighted to be in charge of the legendary stallion. "I'll rub him down and give him a meal worthy of a hero," Longfellow said.

After Beatrice and her companions had showered and changed, and had their wounds properly bandaged, Seamus led the guests of honor to a table in the center of the crowded dining room.

"The Witches' Executive Committee should be here any minute," Teddy said happily before she dug into a bowl of horned-toad chilli.

"Now don't get your hopes up," Cyrus said, his injured shoulder not slowing him down as he reached for a bedbug burger. "You know they won't classify us until after the fifth test."

Beatrice was filling Cayenne's plate when Winifred Stoop arrived at their table, looking more lively and excited than they had ever seen her.

"Won't you join us?" Beatrice asked the older witch.

"I'd love to," Winifred replied, "but I'm working. You see," she added merrily, "I was telling Seamus how I lived all year for this one month at Winged-Horse Ranch, and he offered me a job telling the guests' fortunes. So I'll be staying here now!"

"That's wonderful," Beatrice said sincerely. "And I'm sure you'll be good at your job. Everything you saw about *me* came true."

Winifred's pale eyes rested kindly on Beatrice's face. "And when faced with the decision between good and evil, you made the right choice, didn't you?"

Winifred had just left when Uri and Fairlamb came over to offer their congratulations.

"And guess what?" Fairlamb demanded. She stuck out her left hand and wiggled her fingers, one of which was sporting a ring with a small diamond. "Uri and I are *engaged!*"

Just then, Paxton wandered over to the table and extended a hand to Beatrice.

"Congratulations," he said quietly, and Beatrice was pleased to see that he was actually smiling. "I'm happy that you proved me wrong."

"Thanks for your help," Beatrice said. "So what will happen to the mines now?"

"Morven will run them," Paxton replied. "She sent a note requesting that I stay on as foreman, and I've decided that I will. The gnomes will have good lives again."

Uri had been listening to their conversation and watching Paxton covertly. Now he cleared his throat and looked Paxton in the eye.

"I blamed you for what happened to Dominy," Uri said gruffly, "but I was wrong. It was his decision to go up on that mountain. And as for what I said about you working for Dally Rumpe—"

"Dally Rumpe is gone," Paxton said evenly, and reached for Uri's hand.

Beatrice was smiling as she watched the two old friends shake hands. Then she realized that the room had suddenly gone quiet. Glancing around, she saw heads turned toward the door, and her own eyes darted in that direction. She could hardly believe who was standing there! It was Dominy Griffin, appearing tentative and a little frightened, his hood thrown back to reveal his poor ravaged face and that head of shining hair.

A startled cry pierced the silence. Then Beatrice saw Joy moving like a sleepwalker toward Dominy, and Dominy limping to meet her. In the next instant, they were reaching out their arms and then holding each other. Joy was sobbing now, staring into Dominy's face and saying his name over and over. Dominy's eyes looked suspiciously bright, and he was gripping her so tightly his arms seemed to tremble.

Then Seamus was making his way through the crowd toward the couple. When he reached them, he wrapped his arms around them and buried his face against Dominy's shoulder.

When Beatrice was finally able to tear her eyes away from the trio, she noticed that lots of other people were looking pretty emotional. Uri was wiping his face furiously as he strode across the room to greet his friend, and Paxton was close on Uri's heels, his expression of disbelief changing swiftly to one of joy.

"Wow," Teddy said softly. "Is this terrific or what?"

Across the table from Beatrice, Miranda was sniffling. Beatrice did a double take. Yes, her cousin definitely had tears in her eyes.

"You're such a softy," Beatrice said, smiling.

"Must be the company I've been keeping," Miranda grumbled, and proceeded to wipe her eyes with her napkin.

Beatrice looked back at Dominy and saw that Joy and Seamus were leading him tenderly to their table, with Uri and Paxton following closely behind. Then Seamus's head pivoted in Beatrice's direction, and he was suddenly hurrying across the room toward her.

"You brought him back," Seamus said as he reached the table, tears streaming down his face. He took Beatrice's hands between his own and squeezed them tightly. "He said you convinced him to come home. How can I ever thank you, Beatrice? When I think about how harsh I was with you—"

"It doesn't matter," Beatrice cut in hastily. "I'm just happy for all of you."

"We're going to take good care of him," Seamus said, his voice suddenly fierce, "get him strong again. And you'll have to come back—all of you," he added, his face breaking into a smile as he looked around the table. "For a real vacation. On me."

"We'll take you up on that," Ollie said cheerfully.

After Seamus had left to rejoin his son, Beatrice was dabbing at her eyes, feeling almost giddy with happiness, when Ira Skelly appeared at her elbow. He looked so woebegone that Beatrice nearly felt sorry for him.

"My trip here has been a failure," Ira said mournfully. "I didn't help you—and then—" He glanced over at Joy's table, where she and Dominy were talking quietly with their heads bent close. "Well, anyway, it hasn't turned out the way I had hoped at all."

Beatrice was afraid that her tutor was going to burst into tears, so she said quickly, "I made it impossible for you to tutor me," which was certainly true, "and you did get some research done, didn't you?"

"Well—yes," Ira agreed. Then he perked up a little as he added, "And I just received a letter from the Witches' Institute. They're offering me a fellowship to continue my studies on the effects of prolonged stress on witches."

"What an honor!" Beatrice exclaimed. "So why are you moping around?"

Ira drew himself up and peered down at her with his customary expression of superiority. "Who's moping?" he demanded. "But I don't have time to chat, now. I have to pack! They want me back at the Institute right away."

As she watched Ira make haste for the door—once again, his old pompous self—Beatrice just shook her head. "I hope I never have to see that witch again," she said passionately, and reached for a devil dog.

"From what Ira tells me, you weren't the most cooperative student," came a voice from behind Beatrice.

It was a voice that she had come to know well.

When Beatrice stood up and turned around, she found herself looking into the amused hazel eyes of Dr. Featherstone. Dr. Meadowmouse, Peregrine, and the rest of the committee were clustered around her, and standing slightly apart was Dr. Thaddeus Thigpin, Director of the Witches' Institute. His pale blue eyes, under bushy white eyebrows, were regarding Beatrice with their usual ferocity, but Beatrice thought there was something different about him this time. Then she realized what it was: He was smiling. It was only a faint smile—and a little uneven, as if his lips weren't used to curving up that way—but it was definitely a smile.

Beatrice blew her bangs aside and gave him a tentative smile in return.

"So you've managed to pass the fourth part of the test," Dr. Thigpin said gruffly. "Astounding!"

"And without using Dally Rumpe's evil spells," Dr. Meadowmouse pointed out as he beamed at Beatrice.

"Yes, well—I should *hope* not," the Institute director snapped. Then his craggy face softened just a hair and he said to Beatrice, "You've demonstrated that a witch— even a Reform witch, with no particular talent for magic—can be successful without resorting to unscrupulous behavior. You've shown that you have integrity, Beatrice Bailiwick."

"Not to mention courage," Aura Featherstone added.

"And perseverance," Peregrine squeaked, then ducked back behind Dr. Featherstone.

"As have your friends," Dr. Featherstone said, her eyes sweeping over Teddy, Ollie, and Cyrus, and finally coming to rest on Miranda. "I'm happy that you finally decided whose side you're on, Ms. Pengilly," she said softly.

Miranda's face flooded with color.

Dr. Thigpin waved his hand impatiently. "Enough of this chitchat! Let's get on with it so we can eat."

Dr. Featherstone gave him an exasperated look and then turned back to Beatrice.

"We've come to congratulate you," the older witch said, "and to tell you that you'll be going to Bromwich's castle next. Around Halloween, I should think."

"The last part of the test," Ollie murmured.

Hearing these words sent a shiver up Beatrice's spine. *The last part.* Was it really almost over?

When Seamus came to show the Witches' Executive Committee to their table, everyone went back to eating. Except Miranda.

"Um—Beatrice," Miranda said, seeming oddly hesitant. "I want to give you something."

Beatrice looked up in surprise as Miranda extended her hand across the table. In her palm was a silver pentagram like the one Beatrice had found in her cellar. In its center glowed a small ruby.

Beatrice's eyes darted to Miranda's face and then back to the silver charm. "You're giving this to me?" she asked in confusion.

"The ruby came from the Bailiwick mines more than three hundred years ago," Miranda said softly, "long before Dally Rumpe's time. It signifies love and good deeds. I want you to have it. You've earned it."

Miranda dropped the pentagram into Beatrice's hand, and Beatrice just stared at it, too overcome to speak.

"All the Bailiwicks wear rubies," Miranda continued, her sharp-edged voice and manner resurfacing, as if one tender moment at a time was all she could handle. She reached inside her T-shirt and pulled out a pentagram identical to Beatrice's. "They say that Bromwich used to wear the largest ruby ever found in the Bailiwick mines."

"Maybe we'll get to see it," Cyrus said, "when we go to his castle."

Teddy glanced at Miranda. "Will you be horning in on that trip, too?" she asked dryly.

"I wouldn't miss it," Miranda answered.

"Good," Beatrice said. And meant it.

She had come to realize that Miranda Pengilly was a good witch to have on your side.

After they were back home, Ollie started tutoring Beatrice in American history. One afternoon he was surfing the Witch World Web while Beatrice was taking a practice quiz.

"I can't believe it," Ollie muttered. Then he laughed out loud.

Beatrice glanced up from her history book. "What is it?"

"You've got to see this for yourself," he said, grinning.

Looking over Ollie's shoulder at the computer screen, Beatrice saw that he was on a popular auction site. One of the ads leaped out at her.

RARE BEATRICE BAILIWICK MEMORABILIA!
*Four hairs. Authenticated. A unique addition to
your collection, or give them as gifts.*